SOMETHING ABOUT THE ANIMAL

Something About the Animal

stories

Cathy Stonehouse

BIBLIOASIS

FIRST EDITION

Library and Archives Canada Cataloguing in Publication

Stonehouse, Cathy
    Something about the animal / Cathy Stonehouse.

Short stories.
ISBN 978-1-897231-98-2

    I. Title.

PS8587.T674S64 2011   C813'.54   C2011-900985-4

Cover photo: "Untitled" from the series *The Woman Who Is A Horse* by Gabrielle de Montmollin

Readied for the Press by John Metcalf

Canada Council for the Arts   Conseil des Arts du Canada

Canadian Heritage   Patrimoine canadien

ONTARIO ARTS COUNCIL
CONSEIL DES ARTS DE L'ONTARIO

Biblioasis acknowledges the ongoing financial support of the Government of Canada through The Canada Council for the Arts, Canadian Heritage, the Book Publishing Industry Development Program (BPIDP); and the Government of Ontario through the Ontario Arts Council.

PRINTED AND BOUND IN CANADA

For Wayne

Contents

Among the dead may be counted also
those animals that were not devoured

—Elias Canetti

Memory is an action:
essentially it is the action of telling a story

—Pierre Janet

Beryl Takes a Knife

B ERYL TAKES A KNIFE and scores vehemently along the
dotted line. Beside her on the kitchen table are the other
supplies she bought last month: a large bag of orange-painted
hedgerow and a OO/HO gauge pack of assorted pedestrians.
She has decided it will be October on this, the "farm" side of
her village. Around the pond it will be June, and in the
church graveyard, early April. She was hoping to fit winter in
somewhere, but short of adding an extension to the school
playground, there's no room. Perhaps, thinks Beryl, her ham-
let's microclimate only features three seasons. Who needs
snow anyway?

3:15, 4:45: the time the church clock tells might as well be
now or never. Beryl has inked its hands in at a quarter to two.
That was the time Derek walked out two weeks ago, saying he
wanted a divorce. Beryl hasn't seen him since, although there
have been messages.

Forty miles distant, the city he calls from is a tawdry con-
stellation, its citizens Martians, green-skinned yobbos with
lager cans instead of eyes. Whatever it is Derek's up to there,
Beryl need not concern herself with it. Thankfully contact
cement seals up relationships immediately and offers no
opportunities for doubt: a wall is joined to a wall and there it
will stay, the construction of buildings, even ones fashioned
out of cardboard, a matter of optimism, if not blind faith.
Soon her model farmhouse will be complete and take up its
place beside a small copse of copper beech trees. Beryl will

then grass over the adjoining field with mid-green flock and arrange upon it three miniature Shire horses. She can already see herself doing it, in her mind's eye.

It's understandable he isn't satisfied. A man like Derek needs a rose on his arm, something fresh and pretty to display. In the past two years she's wilted, become like one of those mannequins draped in stained shawls that startled her back into smoking that very first shift. She was working at the Cotton Museum. The figurines were supposed to add authenticity, but no one wants to eat surrounded by grief. Eventually the manager ordered them returned to the 1850s and the tea shop redecorated in contemporary style. Yet something lingered on, an eerie coldness: Beryl feels it again, now, suddenly, as if it's been lying dormant in her soul.

As soon as I've finished the gables, she tells herself, praying they don't rip and buckle like the last ones, I'll put the chimney on and secure it with paper clips and then that's it for the day. Out in the real world, it's a quarter past three on a June school day, and down the road outside, children are beginning to stream home.

"Can you play out?" calls a high-pitched voice.

"Yeah, course!" another answers.

Beryl shudders, sticks her fingers in her ears. How she hates living near a school! She told Derek she couldn't bear it, but he insisted it was a wonderful location, close to the shops yet away from the busy main road. She'd soon get used to the parents and their minivans blocking the crescent for a half hour, morning and night. At the time, Beryl couldn't decide if he meant to be cruel, deliberately not mentioning the thing she was most afraid of – kids. Either way, three months after they moved Beryl gave notice. The panic attacks had just become too intense. Six months later she was even gasping in Woolworth's, sliding like a fish down the side of a mirrored pillar until she lay at the bottom, grasping its base. The face that stared back became the self she fears, a cringing caricature of utter ridiculousness. Better to stay indoors and paint sheep.

Beryl pulls her blouse down firmly, tucks it back into the waistband of her trousers. These stretch shirts have a real tendency to ride up, perhaps because of all the weight she's lost. It's not been regained even after two weeks of toast and jam. At least she's not fat. Derek will be back, she repeats to herself. Give him a week or two.

A mobile phone beeps crassly from the road outside. Beryl bends lower over the table, desperate to disappear but then a volley of gravel shatters against the window and from between the plastic slats two young girls and a young man grin manically up at her, the words they yell beyond her understanding, something like "emo" then "respect."

He said he'd done everything he could to help her recuperate but he couldn't stand it any longer, doing all the errands, fending off enquiries, holding the fort.

He said his sister Deirdre swore it was Beryl's fault: she *wanted* to hide, *wanted* to live like a prisoner. And Deirdre should know: she worked with the mentally ill. Derek, Beryl has deduced, is a new man, all "codependence" and "Higher Power," attending meetings left and right, or so he says. How can she trust a man who has changed so completely? He could have joined the Moonies or turned homosexual. Even a torrid affair is on the cards. Last night before sleep she glimpsed him in a retro kaftan, strolling the Golden Mile, hash pipe in hand.

Of course, she will admit, this is all conjecture. In his last message he said he'd come by next week, pick up some groceries and leave them at the front door. He also said if she agreed to treatment – real therapy, not just bottles of Valium

– he'd move back in. Deirdre has given him great tips on Being Supportive. But Beryl doesn't want to see a shrink.

For one thing, there's her illegitimate son – no longer a baby now, thirty-two last March. She used to mark his birth-date on the calendar with a black dot as small as a zygote, a glint in a girl's eye, a dot invisible to Derek, who has trouble with his eyes, but then came the fateful note from Canada: *All those years, he never asked … but now he's expecting one of his own.* This year there's no dot on the calendar. Instead, a scrap of paper pokes shyly up out of an atlas.

Vancouver: Beryl looked it up with trembling hands. A city on the edge, close to a border, about as far from here as it gets. What were its buildings like? What were its trees? Despite the miles, she felt the pressure of the boy's gaze, turned towards her now after so long, became breathless and jumpy again just thinking about it.

The rape took place in a tiny room, a wardrobe, really. It was the summer she turned twelve; she was already fertile and the smell of mothballs and suntan lotion mingled with the sticky ectoplasm of semen sent her to another world filled with revenants and half-naked shoe salesmen she has never quite left, although her mother told her she must move on – her imperious mother, now dead, who arranged her removal that Christmas to the farm near Ottawa where Beryl gave birth to a red-faced, squirming gargoyle and vomited maple syrup back into snow: reexamining the map, the pained face of the doctor who stitched her up so delicately as if she were a ruined vase returns to question her. *Why didn't you tell anyone?*

"Beryl?" calls a man's voice through the letterbox. A wisp of nicotine uncurls down the hall.

The farmhouse is finished, its paperclips applied, but one wrong move and she could ruin it completely. Wet glue is frighteningly unstable. Perhaps she should retreat to the living room, where Derek's things are still in boxes. Her first indication that something was wrong was when she stumbled upon him folding his sports jackets and laying them in little parcels across the bed. Upon questioning he announced that he was going away for a while, a little holiday – to Yorkshire, perhaps. An hour and several cardboard boxes later, the outlook was bleaker: Derek stated he was leaving indefinitely; by late afternoon, conjuring quotation marks, he needed "space."

Might the spare room count? How about the garden shed? Beryl pleaded, falling to her knees but Derek's mind was made up. At a quarter to two, he adjusted his tie in the mirror, pecked her on the cheek then closed the door.

So far the boxes have remained untouched, transformed by superstition into monuments, a kind of mystic henge she tiptoes through morning and evening on her journey to and from their bed. Now prostrate on the settee beneath a rug it's as if she's lying in a New Age force field. Derek's Argyle socks and filofaxes hum threateningly around her like alien spaceships. If only they would return to earth.

"Beryl?" The letterbox slams shut.

What will happen to the garden?

When she left the bank her plan had been to open an attraction, lay it out across the front lawn. Derek had just been laid off from his job as station master, now that the company had introduced self-serve: sleek, digital ticket dispensers that required maintenance only once a week. People pay money to view attractions and she still had her pride, was determined to provide herself and Derek with a source of income, albeit one that did not necessitate her leaving the house. Her original goal, she admits, was overambitious: a scale model of England circa 1972. Since Derek left, she has scaled back, is focusing instead on three dioramas, each entitled *The England That Could Have Been*. She still believes she can find a way to display them. One can go in the hall, another in the living room, the third in the kitchen, with perhaps a tea shop situated out back. Tourists often stop off for meals, en route to the Lake District: she could put a sign up on the motorway: *Cream Teas and Miniature Propaganda*. The turn-off leads straight past her house.

Perhaps the boy will come, when he visits England. She pictures a tall, lean fellow with a charming accent, perhaps a tartan shirt and beavertail hat, or else a nice blue suit and blonde-haired girlfriend. How will she introduce him? As a family friend, who was raised by his grandmother June because his mother, Janice, died in childbirth. She still remembers Janice, a sneering presence whose neat colourless bob glistened like ice. Perhaps Janice did die at nineteen, but not in childbirth. Perhaps one February her boyfriend Wilbur drove his car, with her in it, off the road. Either way, surely the boy will come when June finally tells him his mother is English and he adopted, not hers, and when he does, Beryl will impress him with her resourcefulness, her skill at rendering scenes from outside time.

"Beryl – is that you? Are you in there?"

"Let's go home, Dad," mutters a teenager. "She's a fuckin' witch."

The Cotton Museum is closed now, amalgamated into the Memory Centre, where high-tech displays catalogue suffering in all its conveniently obsolete forms: the rattle and whirr of spinning jennies, the crack of slave whips, holograms of mill overseers striking child labourers, fake X-rays of spines deformed by overwork. There is a giant, cast-bronze plague rat in the café and gift shop, an impressionist tuberculosis microbe outside each toilet. Beryl could work there again, perhaps as a model maker. If she did, they might even sponsor her display. The day she left the bank she stood outside and experienced a moment of terrifying blankness: the enormity of everything pressing down upon her, squeezing her as if she was just being born. The rained-on streets, the multitude of bodies, the litter of dog shit, crisp packets and credit card receipts, of price tags still attached to plastic wands: all this so blessedly foreign to her now. Some days she opens the back door and takes a few steps, inhales the strange air, but mostly just peers through windows at the tiny, ordered world that still inspires her, the one of begonias, old roses and herb beds that Derek so recently kept up.

"Derek? Derek!" The wool is wet and hairy against her face. "Where are you?" Some days it's as if he's just stepped out and will be back in two shakes of a lamb's tail, laden with sausages, sponge mops, *Masterpiece Theatre* videos, bags of fake foliage. Other days, Beryl's convinced he's given up on her, abandoned his marriage vows and decided to make a go of it as a single man: reading Tarot cards, working in a record shop. The world's your oyster when you can go outside. On those days she weeps. It's not like she hasn't tried: that first visit to the surgery, sitting sweating on the edge of her chair while Dr. McVitie waited and swallowed, his jagged Adam's apple almost piercing the skin of his neck. *And how is your sleep, Mrs. Johnson?* Like being dead, Beryl had answered wistfully. She'd gone back two or three times, shuffling toe to heel, her back against walls, but the journey was too much and anyway the pills were all she wanted, little blue capsules of powdered love she tucks into boxes and corners all over the house in case a moment of doubt overcomes her suddenly. Dr. McVitie seems not to care. He speaks to her over the phone every three months or so, a brief interview that usually ends with an embarrassing question or two about her sex life.

Derek then collects her pills and brings them home to her, in lieu of flowers; in two days she is going to run out.

There's a rapping at the front door. The letterbox reopens: "Beryl? Beryl Rutherford? Come on out now! Please!"

She knows who it is: Uncle Stu of course, Stuart Harley to his business associates, accompanied perhaps by teenage grandchildren. A pale, flabby man with red-rimmed eyes whose hands and arms grow shit-brown splatters of freckles after even brief exposure to the sun: when her mother first brought him home, Beryl thought he had some terrible illness. When he moved in, along with his shoe samples, cardboard display units and winning smile Beryl was ten and from then on was forced to wear orthopedic boots, not because she needed them but because they made her stand tall and stand out. *It's important,* her mother said, *to get noticed.*

Thinking of it now, one of the main reasons she married Derek was because he could disappear in a crowd. Unassuming and average, he made space available for her to be special, just stayed still and held her gaze until suddenly everything she did became interesting. He also didn't mind screwing in the dark. The built-in wardrobe had a light, a naked bulb that polished Uncle Stu's head into an angry planet and Beryl didn't want to examine it too closely in case she too suddenly went into orbit. Derek kindly closed the curtains and put the doorstop under the door, which Beryl enjoyed because it meant she didn't have to wear make-up and also she could cry without her husband noticing. When Dr. McVitie examined her once and asked if she'd ever had a baby she slammed her legs together accidentally kicking him in the face. There was nothing she could do. She was simply infertile. The birth control pills went secretly into her jewelry box, popped out of their blister packs, intermingled with loose beads, a month's worth of privacy at a time.

"Uncle Stu – is that you?" No answer.

After June's letter arrived she started scanning phone books. It had been thirty years, but the name of his company was burned into her consciousness: Step Right Up Elevated Shoes Incorporated. After Beryl's mother had thrown Stu out, not for impregnating Beryl but for spitting out Beryl's mother's beef stroganoff, her ex-stepfather had risen rapidly up the corporate ladder and eventually taken over the company. He had also married and had two children, who were technically Beryl's son's half siblings, she realized. When she called Uncle Stu she would have to mention this. *All in good time*, as her mother would say.

"Beryl, my love: how are you? How's your mother? Still making that lasagna?"

"She's dead, Stu. She died ten years ago."

"Oh dear, what a shame, lovely lady, still, time is money as they say and I am at work so what can I do you for?"

"I … wondered if you'd like to meet me."

"Meet you? Course I would. Trouble is I'm off to L.A. in three weeks … course I've got a chauffeur now, fleet of cars … what's this about, anyway?"

"It's to do with my mother."

"Left me a fortune, did she?"

"She took some photographs."

The line goes dead for a moment while Uncle Stu regains his composure. "All right, all right," his voice slightly quieter now, "Don't get your knickers in a twist. How much do you want?"

"It's not about cash, Mr. Harley. I want to see you."

After some negotiating, during which Beryl implies she is somehow handicapped, confined to a wheelchair perhaps (the last thing she wants him to know is that she's afraid) Stuart Harley agrees to pop over after dark one evening, just for a few minutes, provided Beryl can guarantee she'll be alone. She guarantees instantly, solitude now her permanent condition. They agree on this Thursday, at 10:30 p.m.

Beryl approaches the front door with trepidation. Should she limp? Perhaps if he asks she can say she is having a good day or that her scooter is parked out the back or else in the shop for emergency repairs. Hopefully he just won't notice. Meanwhile there may be at least one grandchild with him. What if he or she looks like the boy? And what will happen when Uncle Stu sees her, middle-aged now, with poor posture and badly dyed hair, nothing like the willowy schoolchild, glossy in tightly-braided pigtails who opened her bedroom door that early evening and welcomed him in with a flash of her braces, her leg? He'd never looked at her before or since, barely seemed to notice until she slipped her socks off, at which point he began examining her insteps. It was true she had been jealous of her mother, hated her really, had wanted to prove she too existed as an entity, was in fact a *force to be reckoned with,* but this was hardly what she had intended, being swooped upon like Leda by the swan, led by her elbow into the closet where her Sindy doll had only last night received a pencil tattoo, noticing how aroused she was by Uncle Stu's caresses, his hand on her cunt, his dear-dear's and there-there's culminating in an excruciating coitus during which she roasted on a spit, oh it was hot in there, in here, the sun once again far too close, the linoleum beneath her feet like tarmac turned sticky as the good doctor cut the cord and handed him to her, Uncle Stu in miniature, rooting for her breast, latching on with razor-sharp gums. *One last good push,* the doctor instructs, his face turned away as the truth slips out, slimy and breathless until the panic rises up, engulfing her like a riptide yet somehow she manages to dance above it, a seabird jagged in its progress towards the horizon, at which point she must reply to June, it is a bit late, too late perhaps, but her aunt is slow and methodical in her habits and may not have decided anything – the boy should be told, should not be told, she is walking so slowly now, practically backwards, forever ambivalent, each whitish-pink petal around that trillium the June she and Derek traveled to Canada supposedly on a whim, Beryl at the helm of a massive rental car, she still drove then, cruising wide roads with no apparent obstacles towards the farm then suddenly away, muttering, *Oh dear, it must be the wrong address*. Derek shrugging his shoulders, smoothing the skin on the back of her hand as she gripped the steering wheel, suggesting they make straight for Niagara Falls, the white-blond head of the boy pushing up from a green field seen in the rear-view mirror becoming a speck of spray now caught in her hair, the roar of rage no one heard as she bent in towards him, her lover, her nemesis – whichever way she looks, the house stares back, its absence of mirrors proof its walls are coterminous with her own skull's.

"Beryl, please answer!" Perhaps it isn't Stu. Perhaps it's her baby. Beryl closes her eyes, imagines hard.

In the first scenario, lovers cavort in a field dotted with May blossom in the same instant that smocked villagers scythe corn, all their faces ever so slightly reddened by the cider that cools in stone flagons in the nearby stream, and there is no separation between the seasons, or at least only a modest few inches, sufficient to allow the foliage to thicken like her own hair and then thin; she has named this diorama *The Forest of Arden*, and it represents England before the Fall. There is no winter here and there are no bomb sites. The churchyard's grass is smooth and there are no graves.

In the second scenario, people of rainbow colours chat amiably atop glistening high rises while on a carefully-tended rhombus of grass, children play. Each gleaming wall sports a

21

mural, and the street below is busy with police cars and fire trucks, health visitors, social workers, their identity badges worked up from lines of newsprint. This diorama represents the Sixties entirely devoid of demonstrations and she has called it simply *The Estate*.

The third scenario causes her the most anguish. A post-Apocalyptic, burned-out landscape pocked with makeshift graves and ashy hovels, its ravaged surface was created in a fugue state, one she woke up from smeared with black enamel paint. This diorama represents the Future and she has named it, tentatively, *Us*. After viewing it, patrons who feel so moved may make small monetary donations to respected charities; perhaps this might win her some media attention. Perhaps then she can forget the Kodak polaroids she took the following night of her mother and Stuart, humping in bed with Halloween masks on. Bloodied, hacked-off limbs are stacked in one corner of the base board, while at the other couples of various species, genders and ages embrace; between them has been carved out a massive crater. Through it she can see her slippered feet: navy plush moccasins distorted by bunions glimpsed through a hole at the centre of the Universe.

Hurriedly she returns to her model village, the rustic centerpiece of *The Forest of Arden,* into which she intends to move as soon as practicable, as soon as Derek and she have learned to shrink. Creeping across the landing in her slippers, still sore from the previous afternoon, she did not know what time it was or why exactly she had her new camera with her, the one Uncle Stu had given her for her twelfth birthday, except that she needed an explanation, an instant fact she could wave in his face as to why he should marry her and not her mother, but it all went wrong and anyway never happened, is only a nightmare or fantasy that recurs too often, recurs once again as she picks up the knife she left on the kitchen table, a stainless steel Exacto, snaps the last blunt, glue-encrusted blade off and extends a new one, shuffles her way to the front door and grasps the knob.

Her beloved terror: a membrane so very thin she could have torn it horseback riding. Instead an intensity of sunlight blinds her. Then suddenly, inevitably, her eyes clear: five foot eleven, fair-haired with blue-grey eyes, dressed in some sort of uniform, her son's shoulder blades are wings that almost open as he raises his arms to hug her then fold again as he offers her his hand.

"Beryl Rutherford?" His voice husky, piercing in its intimacy – how could she have thought it would all end badly? Now she is in Arden, or is that Eden. All is love, powdered love and forgiveness –

"Come this way, dear. Dr. McVitie called us."

Now, where has she heard that? At the Memory Centre? The sound of someone finally taking control – as the bubble bursts Beryl opens her fists and the Exacto knife falls, spearing the Welcome mat. A bald paramedic picks it up and pockets it. No doubt he will use it later to cut the cord.

Floaters

ALLAN WAKE is a tall, thin man with down-turned eyes and a mouth permanently hidden by fluff. Aline bumps into him on her way to the pool. He's handing out leaflets.

"May I interest you in Ayurveda?"

She does not say yes, but neither does she say no.

His leaflets promise eternal life, provided the reader pays $49.95 for a two-volume set of ancient Indian recipes, colour-coded for body type. Aline skim-reads as she rolls out her beach towel. She has time on her hands, now that she's dropped religion. Six years ago she converted from Judaism to Catholicism followed swiftly by Sufism then onto Goddess worship only to return to Judaism by way of Buddhism, but these days it just doesn't seem worth the work. Once upon a time, many years ago, Allan made a pass at her during Aikido (she was Sufi then but having balance problems), his smile revealing even, yellowish teeth. It took her several minutes to disentangle. Perhaps if she hadn't she would now be the mother of Shiva. Instead she has Blake, who at fourteen rarely speaks except to say "bozo."

Aline's current life path is dental assistance, suctioning spit out of people's mouths while making reassuring shapes with her eyebrows: it's all about communication, really: knowing what Susan wants before she speaks. Dr. Susan Solari, lesbian paintball enthusiast, who prides herself on the speed of her extractions. Life could be worse. The two of them moving in synchrony, swabbing and drilling, making the world a safer place to eat nuts in. Blake's dad, Freeman, is in real estate. He sells fixer-uppers that cannot be fixed. Freeman's favourite sayings: Life is too short to be honest. Whenever you tell the truth, you kill a dream. The truth he told Aline was unexpected. He likes to wear pantyhose and high-heeled shoes, but that was never a secret between them. Rather, his affair with her sister, who died at 35 of uterine cancer, blew up in their face when Sandy's diagnosis caused her to go on a confessional rampage. Freeman had said he wanted to tell Aline first.

Blake still blames his mother for the break-up. He thinks his dad is a cool dude, Aline a bore. Freeman calls at odd hours to deliver flowers, hidden amongst them clues to a secret address at which Freeman will meet Blake and give him money. Aline follows at a distance in her Toyota, picks up Blake and takes him to the bank. She insists he put the cash in a trust fund. This is Freeman's idea of child support.

There are other struggles. Once, when Blake was five he asked for a dress. He said she had a bunch so why couldn't he? Unable to think of an answer, Aline said yes, which meant taking him down to the Mental Health thrift store at 11 a.m. on a dark, wet Monday morning, when all the other kids were at school. She figured it would do him no harm. And for all she knew it was entirely genetic; saying no would only screw him up. But when they got there, Blake changed his mind and said he wanted a Batman cape. When there was none he lay down on the pockmarked carpet and screamed until she had to drag him out by his hood. Part of it ripped off. Parenting mistake #3,247: Do not agree to buy something whimsical and frivolous, especially on school time.

When she told Freeman, he just rolled his eyes. "I can't believe you'd let him run you like that."

"I was just trying to be supportive."

"Overanalyzing is what you were doing: reading too much into a simple request."

"So did you have a dress?"

"What?"

"When you were five?"

"What do you think?"

Looking back, it was all so ridiculous: she had worked hard to be open-minded only to find herself taken advantage of. In the last months before Sandy died, Freeman visited her sister often, staying overnight at her house and the hospital and making no secret of their continued passion. Being with Sandy taught him what really mattered. This is what he told her. What could she say? That obviously she, Aline, did not matter? Swallowing her pride she bought them take-out and dropped it outside the door and when the time came washed Sandy's body, dressed it in a sweater Freeman bought.

At the funeral Freeman wept. Yet as Sandy's coffin was lowered into the ground and he gripped Aline's hand and whispered *I love you*, she felt herself soften and that night they made love. The feeling of grace and forgiveness lasted until breakfast, after which Freeman went out for a run, came home with a brand new wig and began packing up his CD collection. While Aline ploughed through mountains of tragic paperwork, returned Sandy's mail and sealed up thank-you cards, her husband emptied his wardrobe, ordered a U-Haul.

When Aline finally moved her clothes back into the built-in wardrobe, they only took up a quarter of its space. There were not enough outfits, too many jangling hangers. So one night, after putting Blake to bed, she decided to turn the empty part into a shrine. The following weekend after soccer practice she and Blake visited the local Bible store and came home with armfuls of tacky sculpture, plaster virgins, crucified Christs, a couple of brightly coloured prints of icons. It wasn't long before Aline was kneeling before them. She never thought she'd get any response. But exactly two years to the day after Freeman left she opened her front door to discover a woven basket filled with artisanal loaves, a whole wild salmon and two chilled bottles of cabernet sauvignon.

Learning of her conversion over coffee, Freeman laughed until he choked. Nevertheless, he accepted her invitation to share in God's bounty. At that time Blake lived exclusively on peanuts, claiming he had the opposite of an allergy – if he went for an hour without eating one his throat swelled – so later that day Aline smeared peanut butter onto slices of sourdough and fed them to him underneath the table, where he soothed an imaginary dog that was terrified of faces, and polished off half the salmon with her estranged husband, whose red silk dress reminded her of choirboys. And in that way began her spiritual life.

So much for God, the Beloved, right action, right thinking. Her current obsession is far less demanding, yet still he drives Aline round the bend. He never comes to the house or leaves her a voicemail, just calls every now and again, on the off-chance she's home. When Blake answers, the man in question is reticent. "Bozo," says Blake. "Mum, it's your bozo boyfriend."

"He's not my boyfriend," says Aline, but it doesn't wash. Blake hands her the phone, the non-boyfriend chuckles.

"How's tricks," he begins, or puts on a German accent. "So vat I can do today to afoid gettink gum disease?"

You could say he is immature. You could say he is ugly. Ideally she would either like him assassinated or else to ask him out on a proper date. But how can a woman of thirty-eight invite a tattooed window cleaner of twenty to a movie or a concert without seeming evil, or being refused? When he asked for her number she was half undressed, rubbing sun-screen into her wrinkly shoulders. Her heart quickens when she hears his sarcasm, seeping down the phone like white vin-egar, scalding all her openings, even as it cleans.

"So, did you shower this morning?" asks the boyfriend, while Blake stands beside her, doing his chicken dance or winding the neck of his T-shirt tighter and tighter until his face turns red and she's certain he's strangling.

"Call me later, okay?" whispers Aline. There's no use flirt-ing with losers when your son's acting bozo. You have to get in there and make him stop. After cuffing his face she unwinds Blake's T-shirt, carefully smoothes it out across his body, suddenly aware that he is bigger than her.

Aline shivers. She's wearing her new yellow one piece, even though it's overcast. Several huge pregnant women bob in the shallow end, goggled-up lengths swimmers darting between them like fish. Back on solid ground a toddler grimaces while a cod-white man with a shriveled leg limps along the grass. Where are the beautiful? In Whistler of course, hiking through alpine meadows, or working downtown, gazing through glass at empty sidewalks. Allan Wake is still handing out pamphlets beside the turnstile. Aline flips through hers again, understands none of it, and then a dog trots by, all bad breath and mange. This reminds her it's time she got her nails redone. She pictures herself in a new black dress, drumming her scarlet talons against the receiver as Bozo Boyfriend strug-gles for breath between sobs. *Muthafucka.*

Yes, she's a mother, and yes, he's fucked her, although looking back it was more of a fumble, a quick in-and-out behind the hedge. She was feeling unsettled. Susan at work had confided that her girlfriend was transitioning, asked if Aline had any tips for partners. "Freeman's still a man," Aline had responded. "And we're separated." Susan had insisted these were mere technicalities. The two of them had a battle booked for the weekend, and Jocelyn wanted to be introduced as Josh. "Don't let her/him anywhere near your sister, especially if she has terminal cancer," popped out of Aline's mouth and through her face-mask before she remembered that Pat, whose root canal they were busy doing had just been diagnosed with something bad.

Then when she got home, Blake told her he was in a band. "Playing what?"

"I don't know. I haven't decided." They had a gig the following night at 11 p.m. in some bar she had never heard of. "We're called the Republicans."

It was then the man knocked on the door asking for work. He was young and bald, slightly overweight, with a pierced ear and a twitch that affected his right eye. Aline agreed to let him wash the windows and when he was done she went outside and noticed that the lilacs were in bloom. While the TV screeched and exploded, she found herself stripping, the man with his mop in his hand as if it might be needed, perhaps to wipe her breasts off, sluice down her torso, her cutoff jeans around her knees in the shadow of the burgeoning maple, and when they were through she remembered suddenly where she had seen him: back at the pool in Kits, dressed in garish shorts, horsing around with a girl whose buttocks wobbled.

Later she wondered if she was still fertile, just what she was doing, screwing men in the yard while her son watched DVDs, and whether the man had been stalking her since the pool, following her home every Wednesday after she left there until he decided the time was ripe for him to strike. Perhaps he had meant to rape her but she had raped him instead, leaving him with a terrible identity crisis. Either way he still had her phone number, which she had scrawled on a ripped-off section of bus transfer and given to him by way of explanation, along with a bright, distant smile. Would he come back? Would she find herself again under the maple, this time perhaps less desperate, more considerate, or would he arrive in the night with a knife and a glass cutter, ready to make off with her laptop, her life?

Instead, Bozo just phones from time to time, appears at the pool in his board shorts to chat and flirt. "Well I must be off," he will say, with a glance at his cell phone, or at Buttock-wobbler, hovering by the turnstile. Perhaps they think she will eventually fuck them both, turn out to be some benevolent sugar mommy who will fund their nascent careers as spoken word artists. It's fruitless to speculate, but anything is preferable to silence, that horrible buzz that erupts after midnight when all her scheduled programming comes to an end, Blake asleep, his long eyelashes now visible.

Closing his door and lying back down on her bed she finds herself glancing back and forth, trying to catch a glimpse of one of her floaters. One long strand in particular, always just off to the left, drives her nuts the way it slides and glides. Sometimes, lately, she has stopped what she is doing specifically to launch a stealth attack: maybe, if she surprises it, a face, perhaps even a personality, will appear. Her optician insists all she is seeing are shadows but how ridiculous, that a speck of her own eye should act so secretively. One day, she thinks, I will confront the bastard, just stare it down until it dissolves.

Webs of light, dead flies, someone's lost earring: down here nothing means what it would on the surface. As Aline pushes off, the salt water parts and sends waves rolling without obstruction. Her arms are lean and brown but under water they ripple, luminous as tentacles. One day she opened her eyes to observe a child, hovering motionless as if preserved in a jar, burst to the surface, and was almost convinced she had witnessed a miracle. That was back in her Christian phase. Today all that resurrects is her uneasiness, that tightness about the chest she has been avoiding ever since Freeman's postcard from Spain arrived.

It was utter madness, and from a man she's never known to be weird. This despite the ugly dresses, the garish pumps and purses, all of which offend Aline's taste but not her morals, for she is long past even registering her ex-husband's skirts. Let him wear nylons if he likes. It amounts to as much as her penchant for salted pistachios. No, her problem with him goes rather deeper. No matter how bad things get, he insists on an almost fatuous degree of optimism. With the exception of his theatrical, morbid mother, no one around him is ever allowed to be glum.

So when the mail arrived yesterday after breakfast and she saw the snapshot of a beach curlicued by palm trees, all it took was a glance at his florid signature to trigger in Aline the usual sarcastic ripostes: *Having a wonderful time, glad you aren't here, life is GRRREAT and don't you dare tell me otherwise.* It was only while she brushed her teeth that she decided to read it, read the card that convinced her he'd lost his mind.

I went out for a jog yesterday and tripped over a body on the beach. A dead body! Do you get that, Aline? Some poor sod who tried to make it from the Sudan, traveled overland and hopped in a dinghy. They wash up here every day. No one even notices. Gran Canaria: the gateway to Paradise. The gateway to Hell, in his case. Possibly in my case. Help me, love, I think I'm going insane.

"Love" was the word that made her shiver. Spitting out foam, she turned on the overhead light.

I can't stop thinking about it, can't stop imagining what that man must have run from. And how come he drowned before he got a chance to land? Does he have kids? Parents? How could this happen??!

Holding her breath, Aline tries again to imagine it, the life of the man who drowned in crystal-clear water, jumping to avoid detection, or perhaps being pushed. After Freeman's card arrived she went on-line and read several newspaper articles, accounts of refugees arriving by the boatload. An hour passed, then another. Her wrists ached. Men and women, but mostly men, desperate for opportunity, seduced by Europe, its presence so close to their shacks, just a walk and a death away, who cram onto inflatables, cross the Mediterranean – how could she have not known about them before? Men like Freeman perhaps, fatally optimistic. Risk-takers who leave their families, strike out for Paris, only to drown at sea or end up imprisoned. For a moment or two she was with them, but then grew fatigued. The feeling in her chest was of a trapdoor closing. It's sad, she admitted, but what am I to do? Her life was complex enough. She logged off. Suddenly it felt urgent to masturbate. On the other hand, there was that new Belgian chocolatier.

On her way out, she coolly placed the postcard in the recycling. No doubt Allan would have some kind of remedy, an ancient dietary practice to ward off conscience, the invasion of despair from outlying regions. Seven hedgehogs later she felt like barfing. The chocolate store clerk stared at her as if she were an addict, her twenty dollar bill a prescription, something he had to accept because he was obliged to, the hedgehogs down her throat before he'd rung them in.

That night she and Blake ate salad with no dressing and amazingly, Blake did not protest. Instead he talked, and she noticed how his voice broke while he told her about some girl who had passed him in the hallway and muttered "I love you," and how he was not sure if this was a joke. Aline took his hand, told him he was handsome. He laughed back in a new way, a kind of seal bark, and she did not say a word about Freeman's card.

Where is Sandy, she thought, when I need her? Her sister, who stitched women up after their cesareans, who always seemed wise, even while committing sibling adultery. Jesus, Buddha, Mohammed, Aphrodite. Incantations thicken her head: Blessed be, Mogadon tea. Take a couple of Yahweh, call me in the morning. Six months ago, just as she was heading out to a meeting, her Jewish Women's Sexuality Seminar to be exact, a dog stopped in front of her, right on the sidewalk, lifted its leg and peed all over her shoes. They were Campers, brand new and very expensive. It occurred to her then that dogs and cats and squirrels had no time for seminars. Life, to them, was all about piss and shit. Frozen in an attitude of crisis, she allowed the Chihuahua urine to penetrate her uppers, seep into her Thinsulate socks, and by the time it had anointed her ankles every speck of yearning had left her body, and for the first time since Freeman left, she felt at peace. *Screw the Kabbalah.* Turning on her heel, she headed back home, where she took off her shoes and socks and threw them in the garbage. But it wasn't long before she had brand new ones, orange spike heels and snakeskin stilettos perfect for sitting and watching *Seinfeld* reruns in. Shoveling brain-smart popcorn into her mouth, she would sit and scrutinize her thin legs in immense detail. Would they look better in flattering fishnets? How about short shorts, or a sexy sarong? Discovering clothes while remaining chaste was like becoming a female-to-female transvestite. There was no relief.

Today, in her yellow one-piece, slicing through the saltwater towards the deep end, she recites the long-distance number of Freeman's hotel as if it's a mantra, the thought that he is unhappy, that he doubts himself suddenly, enough to lift up her ribcage and separate her vertebrae, provide all the spiritual loft she needs.

Has he finally got it? Or is this card a new kind of trend? Tell the truth and kill a dream. No, something has happened to her ex-husband, something that has never happened to her. Jealous, Aline pictures herself jogging contentedly, arches well supported in athletic shoes, making her way across wet sand – better to run on – and leaping cleanly over the dead man's body, continuing her run without missing a beat. For how much has Freeman ever cared? Oh, it's all very well to have a fit of conscience, now when he lives all alone.

"What are you doing? Have you any idea where you are going?"

"Oh my God," whispers Aline. It's Buttock-wobbler, dripping in a fuchsia bikini. Aged about twelve with bleached blonde hair and a ring through her navel that's obviously infected, she sneers to someone looming beside her. "Josh! Josh? Look who it is!"

"I see, Babe." Bozo appears, tan and relaxed.

"I could prosecute," says Aline, wagging her finger. Yes, that's right, he *is* stalking her. He *is* a rapist! And maybe it's time his girlfriend knew.

"Prosecute me for what?" Josh/Bozo tosses his girlfriend a beer. "You're the cougar."

"How dare you!" Rage rises up in her like a tsunami. Convinced she is about to kill, Aline jumps out of the deep end and onto the grass, then barefoot and wet, breaks into a run, not even slowing down to pass through the turnstile.

"Aline! Aline Bushnell!"

No one has called her that since she was in high school. How old is she again? Aline cannot remember, wipes a tear from her eye as she watches Allan Wake sprint up, his body impossibly muscular even after this long. Just outside the entrance to the pool, where women and men pull out their wallets, their tickets, Allan Wake embraces her crushingly, tips her over onto the lurid grass.

"Allan, Allan I …"

His teeth are no longer yellow. He must have got false ones. His hair smells of ghee and his chin is unshaven, little white prickles between the black. How easy it is, thinks Aline, to forget about facial hair, Allan's moustache a little animal burrowing blindly towards her nostrils. An image of Freeman sears through her mind. Freeman at college, during that Chaucer lecture, the saucy Miller's Tale not enough to rouse Aline from her sleep-deprived stupor until the guy with the bright red Jewfro handed her a message: LOVE, LOVE, LOVE. What is he doing now? Is his plane landing? Who will be there to meet him, to talk him through it, the shock of death, of truth, right there on the beach? Performing some yogic maneuver she didn't know she knew, Aline extracts herself from beneath Allan's body.

"I'm sorry, Allan," she mutters. "I'm not sure what happened."

"It's okay, it's okay." The owner of the little, furry animal picks up his glasses.

She watches him brush the grass off his shoulders, hears him chuckle.

"Wow, you're some lady."

Aline trembles. When did she last eat?

"I shouldn't have presumed. I just, I don't know." He slides his glasses back on. Then he takes them off again. "I guess I kind of wanted to right some wrongs."

"What sort of wrongs?"

"Oh, you know. Well, you don't know." He turns to look at her, glasses-less, deep little indentations beside his eyes. "Let's just say I have some bad karma."

Aline adjusts the seat of her one-piece, suddenly aware how it has ridden up. "Allan. You're a good friend." This isn't strictly true but she says it anyway.

"Thanks, Aline." Allan pauses. "Listen, I think you have *waaay* too much kappa in your system. Try to avoid onions. Eat more yogurt."

"More yogurt?"

"Yep, more yogurt."

"Okay. Do you still do Aikido?" She notices his FREE TIBET T-shirt, ripped at the neckline, wonders what else he has done in his long life.

"No, it's too heat producing. I've taken up golf."

Later on, after they've parted, Aline wanders over towards the beach. For a moment she thinks she sees Bozo and his girlfriend, shouting obscenities at her, but then isn't sure. So she steps into the sand, warm and disabling, and it's there she finally sees it, the thing that has been dogging her for weeks. A sickle-shaped clump of cells, like the beginnings of a human being, that drifts out in front of her eye and for a moment stays there, its expression neither kind nor cruel, simply impassive, like a smile she never knew she had.

A Special Sound

"**S**O, SHALL WE HAVE OUR MEETING?" asks Heather Johnson. I'm sitting under a tree in the playground while Heather stands above me, blocks out the sun. Because of the bomb scare, none of us is allowed to go inside.

We walk to where Julie and Erica are. Julie and Erica are twins except you wouldn't know it. They wear different clothes and everything. Julie has brown hair in bunches, while Erica has yellow hair in a brand-new pageboy.

"Your bum's wet!" says Erica, giggling, when I turn round.

"Yes, it is! Gaynor's bum's wet!"

"Ssh," says Heather, looking suspiciously at the Loud Girls from over her shoulder. "We have to have our Meeting now, if you want to be Members."

Heather sits down, putting her metal leg out in front of her. It's like a big frame around her knee ending in a big ugly boot which none of us is ever allowed to mention. First we get our notebooks out, the 20p ones Heather bought with our first dues. They are very thick and very yellow. "Page one," I write on page one, underlining heavily. Then the date: June 17, 1977.

"Repeat after me," says Heather. It was her idea to start a Secret Society. She is the Captain, or President, while I am the Vice President – or at least until someone older comes along. Heather is older than me, Erica or Julie. She is the oldest girl in our school.

Heather's right hand is up in the air with three of its fingers crossed, each finger stacked up on top of the other: this is our Salute.

"Cross my heart and hope to die, never ever reveal anything, shall I."

"Cross my heart and hope to die, never ever reveal anything, shall I," repeats Erica first, and then Julie. I don't need to. I have already taken my vow, so instead I help to stack their fingers properly.

"Now I have to cut your finger," announces Heather.

"No, you don't!" says Erica.

"Do not," adds Julie, but they are too late because Heather does it anyway, taking out the safety pin she keeps pinned to the top of her knickers, undoing it then reaching for Erica's hand and jabbing the pin's tip into one of Erica's fingertips.

I repeat the necklace prayer inside my head as I press Erica and Julie's fingertips hard against the yellow page. It's the very back page of Heather's notebook. Mine and Heather's blood is on it too. I don't like blood; it makes me feel sick. Julie's finger sticks to the page. I pull it away with a yank.

"So, what's the password?" asks Erica.

"Our password is Buster Keaton." Heather already has busters, but I don't.

"The password's changed," says Heather, kicking me sharply. "The new password is, um, is —"

"Intercourse!" says Julie, giggling first then clapping her hands in shock across the front of her mouth.

"No, that's stupid," says Erica, shoving her sister backwards.

"Okay, the new password is, um," continues Heather, "'myx-oma-tosis.'"

"What's that?" asks Erica.

"It's a disease. It's what the rabbits get in *Watership Down*," I explain, feeling suddenly clever. "It makes them go blind."

"Cross my heart and hope to die, never ever reveal anything, shall I," announces Heather. This is our signal to end the Meeting, so I lift my right hand up in the Salute.

"Cross my heart and hope to die, never ever reveal anything, shall I," she repeats, and we all join in this time, followed by a loud chorus of 'myxomatosis.'

"Remember not to forget the password," says Heather.

"No," I add. I am the Vice President. "Because if you do –"

"If you do," says Heather, "somebody might die."

Just then the alarm goes off again, telling us we're allowed back inside.

The necklace prayer goes like this:

Hey old Mary, full of grace, the law deals with thee. Blessed art thou, a monk's woman, and, blessed tart, the Fruit-of-thy-Loom, Jesus. Hey old Mary, prefer us in us, now and at the arrow of Ardyth.

I know it because my mum said I had to learn it. If I look at her photo with half-closed eyes I can sometimes hear it speak. Mum always sings to me over breakfast. After she's done I go up to my room, sit on my bed and pray and that's when the spy comes. Once upon a time Mum and Dad were called Mr. and Mrs. McManus, I was called Gaynor Elizabeth McManus, and we all lived together in a little terraced house with my three uncles, Michael and Seamus and Col. Uncle Michael had a wart on his nose and Uncle Seamus had extremely sticky-out ears. They were my mum's older brothers. Uncle Col, Mum's favourite brother, was younger. Four years ago, in 1973, Uncle Col died in an explosion. We haven't seen any of them since then.

My mum was very, very pretty. She wasn't fat like me, had auburn hair, liked doing crosswords and was good at baking. Just before she went to heaven she had big, big lumps all over the inside of her body. But the night she died she was very brave, Dad says. She died so fast that even the morning after there was still half a homemade Battenburg cake in the rose-patterned tin for us to finish. I kept a slice, although it's gone all hard now. I keep it wrapped in Happy Birthday serviettes in a worn-out pillowcase under my bed.

When Uncle Col died, he was in pieces. They had to put them all in plastic bags. At the funeral they put his photograph on the coffin, so everyone could remember who he was. Col had red hair and freckles. Once he took me for a ride on his bike.

"Would you like a biscuit?" I've opened a packet of Custard Creams and put six out on a Tupperware plate between me and Dad.

"No, thanks, and only two for you, mind. We don't need you getting any bigger."

I've already eaten four, but I don't say.

"Fucking Brits," mutters Dad, jabbing his smouldering ash toward the telly. Moving across it are wobbly-legged soldiers. They are in a street somewhere back in Ireland. All the soldiers have dirty faces and wear Action Man costumes. Heather Johnson collects Action Men.

"Fucking Brits, get out."

I do my best to change the subject. "Guess what, Dad: we had a bomb scare today. It was really boring, actually. I knew it was a bomb scare because the fire alarm made a special sound. We have two different fire alarms at school now, one for actual fires and one for bombs."

"Shut up I'm watching television."

Blessed art thou. Mum's voice starts up again, reminding me of things I'm not supposed to talk about. On the TV, a woman screams and shakes her fist while another woman wearing a flickering headscarf cries big sobs into her hands. Remember her face, says the spy. It might be important.

"Go to your room, Gaynor. Someone's coming round."

"Who?"

"Auntie Jude."

"Oh, right."

"Go on then."

Dad's new name is Peter. While he is getting ready I accidentally-on-purpose tip the biscuit plate upside down on the carpet. But then I feel scared so I pick the plate back up, making sure to leave some crumbs beside the beige settee.

The TV is still on. Just as Dad comes out of the bathroom, the doorbell rings, the audience laughs, and Auntie Jude is suddenly visible, a blur of red sundress behind the front door's frosted glass. While Dad heads toward it I close the door to my room softly behind me, cram hairy biscuits into my mouth.

When we moved here from Derry, Dad said we were making a fresh start. That meant becoming Protestant. I'd never been inside a Protestant church before, but Dad said it wouldn't really hurt. *It's what Deirdre would have wanted.* Deirdre was my mum. We only went once. Dad ended up making us leave halfway through. He said everyone could smell the incense on us, even though we'd both just taken baths.

Dad has put his Elvis album on and now he's pouring drinks. I try not to listen to him and Auntie Jude talking. *Chink, chink. I love you.* I tap my fingernail against the window to see if it makes the same cold icy noise.

When I am sure they are gone I leave my room and go out in search of the dictionary. It's in the living room next to our other book, *Murder on the Orient Express*. The dictionary is big and keeps slipping out of my hands. "Viral disease causing tumours in rabbits," reads one definition, the other, "copulation of man and woman." What's copulation? "The physical union of male and female persons." I bet my spy would be sick if he ever saw that.

Perhaps I should call Heather Johnson. Heather lives over on the other side of the village. I've never been in it, but I often like to imagine her bedroom: on one wall, an enormous poster of Donny Osmond, lined up against the other, Action Men.

I dial her number.

"Heather," I say into the phone, "Heather, I have a secret to tell you." Heather pays me 2p every time I tell her something true that nobody else in the village knows. "You'll never believe this," I begin, but there's no answer: the line's engaged.

I can't sleep. While Dad and Auntie Jude bump about in Dad's bedroom, I pull my pillow over my head and start to recite the Lord's Prayer. Sure enough, before I've even got to "Wilby Dunn" my spy appears, pulling up the collar of his raincoat as he slips out of his world and into my bed. His angel feathers tickle my face and his gown is wet but otherwise he feels normal. Instead of talking I just stretch out on my stomach. My spy rolls over and begins scratching my back. His fingernails are very sharp, like talons, but he is gentle.

"Gaynor," he says as he scratches, "do not be afraid. My name is Cecil and I bring you glad tidings. Your mother is alive in heaven. Your father will be back to normal soon.

Meanwhile there are things you do not know about but I am a spy sent from Ireland and I know them all because I have a secret tape recorder. I can also read people's minds."

Lying still beside him, I feel relieved. His voice, a bit like Mum's, is very comforting and his wings are warm and dark, like a real duvet. I don't even care when he starts to talk about secrets, about the phone call God has asked him to make. I just close my eyes and drift out with him towards heaven. I bet Heather Johnson has never been this close.

The next morning, before school, Cecil and I manage to sneak into the spare room. Dad's on the toilet. He can't hear us at all from where he is. I pull down the key from its secret hiding place behind the wardrobe. All Cecil says he needs is a peek – at the white gloves, the folded flag, the lucky rabbit's foot, the multicoloured picture of poor crucified Jesus and the shiny black handle of Granddad's gun – to maintain his powers. First we exchange winks and then after we've touched them all and said "hey, old Mary," I lock the metal box again and slide the drawer soundlessly back in.

Later, on my way home from school I stop at the sweet shop and buy a mixed bag of penny chews. I buy fifteen of them, eight Fruit Salads and seven Black Jacks. I like opening the paper they are wrapped in, feeling their sweetness dissolve down to spit in my mouth. I'm just on my fifth Fruit Salad when I turn into our street and get a bit of a shock.

Parked outside our house is a police car: a Paddy wagon. Beside it a group of nosey parkers are huddled together: Sandy Patel, Mrs. H. from two doors down, and two fat women with little babies. I think one of them works at the supermarket.

"What's up, Gaynor, what's happening?" asks Sandy.

I don't reply, just cut across the road to avoid them, ducking quickly in behind our hedge. My last Fruit Salad has shriveled down to a sore spot on the inside of my left cheek. Crouching down I pray, try to summon Cecil. Surely he must know what's going on.

"Gaynor, there you are, love. Come in, come in." Instead of Cecil it's Auntie Jude who answers the door, still in her chemist's overalls, nametag hanging off, hair all rumpled. I follow her big bottom into the front room.

On the coffee table there's a plate of chocolate digestives. I pick one up then put it down quickly, my fingers already melting its outermost edge.

"Hello there," says a grey-haired man in uniform. Dad's sitting opposite him on a chair from the kitchen. Both of them are nursing cups of tea.

"Hello," I say.

"And what's your name?" asks the strange man.

"Gaynor," I answer, sitting down hard on the arm of the beige settee.

Dad's eyes settle on me from behind his glasses. "Go upstairs, Gaynor. Go on," he says, and jerks his head in the direction of the door.

"Okay," I say and do as I'm told, Auntie still hovering in the living-room doorway, fiddling with the solid gold St. Christopher Dad bought her last Christmas when she said she was going to America then never did. The stairs seem extra steep, and I feel like my ears must have stretched from so much listening by the time I reach the door to my bedroom. I open it and then close it, pretend to go in.

From the landing I can hear the middles of words, long, important ones. Sometimes my dad's voice gets loud, too. Is he lying? Heather Johnson asked me once where Derry was. I told her close to Nice, in the South of France.

Hey old Mary full of grace. The law deals with thee.

About a week ago Uncle Seamus knocked on our front door. It was five o'clock in the morning. I ran out on the grass then ran back inside. Uncle Seamus's ears still stuck out but he had a new scar on his top lip and was all dirty.

"By God, you've grown," he said, picking me up then putting me down quickly.

"What the hell are you doing here?" whispered Dad from the hallway.

"I'm in trouble," said Uncle Seamus.

"I bloody know you are," said Dad, dragging him into the kitchen. "How did you find us?"

"Eileen," said Seamus.

"Shit," said Dad. "Well you can't stay here."

"Just the one night," said Uncle Seamus. "I've got a job –"

"I don't want to know," whispered Dad. " I'm out now. Don't you get it?"

"Just the one night," repeated Uncle Seamus, this time with his hand inside his jacket, taking a hold of something in there, which suddenly clicked.

"All right, Seamus, all right," said Dad, "for God's sake."

The next day Uncle Seamus stayed at home while I went to school and Dad went off to work. Then that night I made us Mum's special spaghetti. We ate it in silence. Dad said he didn't want the next-door neighbours picking up on Uncle Seamus's voice. Then I went to bed at nine o'clock after watching telly. Early the next morning, while it was still pitch dark, Uncle Seamus left by the back door wearing Dad's anorak and trainers. I stood watching secretly from between my curtains, until Dad came in and clipped me over the head.

"Thank you very much, Mr. McManus, we'll be in touch," says the grey-haired policeman as he opens the front door finally and lets himself out.

I go downstairs.

"You never told me about this," says Auntie Jude.

"You never asked," answers Dad.

I start dancing tap steps in the living-room doorway, waving my hands around like Shirley Temple, yet neither of them even notices me. *Hey old Mary, pray for us in us.* Auntie Jude just picks at her fingernails while Dad reaches for the bottle he keeps tucked inside the coalscuttle.

"Do you want a cup for that?" I ask.

"Come here, Gaynor," says Dad, holding his arms out. I run into them. "Yes, love," he says. "Yes, that would be very nice."

I go into the kitchen, open the top cupboard and take down a chipped brown coffee cup. I'm on my way back to the living room when I hear a crash.

"God in heaven!" yells Dad. Then I hear another crash, followed by a yell. I go back into the kitchen and put the cup down on the kitchen counter. I don't want to go into the living room if Dad and Auntie Jude are having a fight.

There was a big fight the night we left Derry. Uncle Seamus and Uncle Michael and Uncle Michael's girlfriend Auntie Eileen, and other people I can't even remember all yelling and screaming at each other. I do the same thing now that I did then: pop my fingers up and down on the flaps of my ears. It's like turning the volume up and down fast on a radio, hearing the chopped sound but not actually listening to the words.

Cecil says telling tales is actually holy. I wonder if rabbits dream when they're about to die. In my dream the sun is falling – not setting, but hurtling toward the earth. The roof of our house has been removed and I am staring up into the massive glare of it, a sky-wide sun that's boiling the backs of my eyes. I've been in bed for hours but it's still not dark. On the table beside my bed is a stack of five 10p coins. Equals 50p, equals twenty-five secrets: a pocket money bonus, for keeping quiet. *Cross my heart and hope to die, never ever reveal anything shall I.*

My dad's arms are covered with blond hairs. He has five tattoos, which he keeps covered: "signs of a misspent youth." Heather has never seen her dad except in pictures. He and her mum were never actually married. Apparently he's a Corporal in the British Army. She says he looks exactly like Action Man.

My mum came to England once when she was younger. We still have the recipe book she bought: *Naughty but Nice: The Best of British Puddings and Cakes.* I like to read it sometimes. It has photos of the cakes and puddings. I repeat their names in my head to make myself sleepy: *Madeira, Genoa, Charlotte, Empress, Queen.*

Dad says we should never have moved to England, it was a mistake. We should have moved further, to America. He says as soon as he next gets paid he's going to leave his job at the garage and take me and Auntie Jude to Canada. Or somewhere. Dad says she has just as much of a reason to leave as we do. I thought they'd had a fight, but he says she will come around. And even if she doesn't, Dad says we'll go anyway. Everyone has a right to a future, he says, no matter what they've done in the past.

Dad pokes his head in. "Are you all right there, Gaynor?"

"Yes, Dad," I say as he comes in and sits down on my bed.

"Only I thought I heard somebody crying." He runs his hand softly through my hair.

"No, Dad. I'm okay." I think of the multicoloured picture of Our Lord Jesus Dad keeps locked away with Granddad's gun, because the fact is Dad's tone of voice right now is

49

making me anxious. Did Jesus Himself feel this worried, when He finally arrived at the Arrow of Ardyth?

"I know it's hard to see right now, but all of this, *everything,* is for your mother." Dad's breath smells alcoholic. "She really loved you, you know."

Madeira, Genoa, Charlotte, Empress, Queen.

"Do you know what 'myxomatosis' means?"

"No, love, I don't."

"It's a vile disease causing tumours in rabbits."

"Is that so?" Dad reaches into his pocket for a cigarette while I close my eyes and try to imagine that Mum's there, with us, eating cake and stroking my hair too.

I'm in the playground the following Tuesday morning and for some reason Heather isn't there. So I go up to Karen Purves who's nice and in her class, and ask her if she knows where Heather is.

"You mean you don't know?" she says.

"No."

"Heather Johnson and Robert Kent were caught snogging in the shopping precinct last night by Mr. Beresford." Mr. Beresford is our headmaster. "Heather had her skirt up round her waist."

"What about Robert Kent?" Robert Kent is fifteen at least and goes to the boys' secondary modern. He is ugly and spotty.

"What about him?" asks Karen. "Was he your boyfriend as well?"

"No, of course not." I look away. I once told Heather that Karen Purves was albino, because she has blonde hair and light blue eyes. I also once told Heather that Robert Kent was actually American, except he was wanted by the sheriff so he was living in England just for now.

I didn't think Heather Johnson fancied anyone. Let alone that anyone fancied her.

When the bell rings for registration and we go inside, Heather is standing outside Mr. Beresford's office. We all walk past her on our way to our class. Everyone looks at her, then at me, then back at Heather. No one has mentioned the police car but I'm sure they're thinking about it. Everyone who uses the supermarket's probably heard.

At break-time Heather Johnson's surrounded by girls. Yet by lunchtime everyone's avoiding her. It turns out Robert Kent didn't fancy her after all. Erica and Julie's older brother Martin dared him to kiss Heather in public after Robert had called her "the world's ugliest girl."

Erica and Julie seem to have a lot of other friends now. From the way they laugh when I walk past I doubt that I am one of them. I don't know what that means about our club.

Neither does Heather, who's hiding in the senior girls' toilets. After I finish my sandwich I follow her in there. She's in the middle cubicle, the one with "Bay City Rollers" scrawled in felt-tip pen across the wall.

"Myxomatosis," I say, making the hand signal and holding it under the cubicle door.

"Go away," replies Heather.

"Erica and Julie are stupid," I say. "And so is Martin."

"Leave me alone," she says. I can see her metal boot poking out the side.

"Why didn't you tell me about Robert Kent?"

"Why should I? You never tell *me* anything."

"Yes I do! I told you all about Mrs H., and Auntie Jude, and Karen Purves."

Heather unlocks her cubicle and stomps out, glaring. "My mum told me Catholics breed like rabbits!"

"My dad says that you're a spastic slag!" *Blessed tart.*

"You cow!" Heather kicks me hard in the ankle. I step back, losing my balance, fall down onto the wet tiled floor. I can't see anything for a minute. My ears are ringing. It's the alarm going off again, the one that says it's a bomb scare not a fire. "Walk, don't run!" shouts Mrs. Jervis from somewhere out in the corridor. I don't feel well. My head is throbbing. I think I'm going to be sick.

I hobble over to a toilet just in time for the big sour fountain of jam sandwich remnants that erupts from my stomach to land with a lumpy splatter right in the bowl. Just then the toilets door swings open. It's Mrs. Jervis. "Come on, girls, outside, chip-chop." I wipe my mouth and flush the toilet.

"Come on," she says, and we go out into the corridor, join the others filing onto the school field through the double doors, except I don't stop at the field, I just keep going, hobble on down the path to the main road.

I try to walk fast but my ankle is killing. The sound of the bomb alarm fades. As I'm crossing our road I realize I've left my satchel behind. It had my packed lunch in it. I think about the box of Almond Slices I hid a week ago under my bed. I bought it with my saved-up pocket money. Perhaps when I get home I will have one.

"This is my house," I say, letting myself in. But as soon as my imaginary boyfriend and I enter the living room he gasps out loud. The TV is broken. The settee's been cut and foam is pouring out like batter. The metal box from the spare room is smashed and empty, a twisted mouth biting into the floor. Where's Dad? Is he still at work?

He isn't in his room, and neither is his jacket, although the bag that he was packing is. His photo of Mum is lying on the floor. A drawer has been overturned beside her, spilling English coins across her face. Where is our lucky rabbit's foot? Did somebody steal it? I crawl under the bed, press my fingers into my eyes until all I can see are colours, like petrol on puddles and then in about a second Cecil arrives. We fly together back into the living room. The ceiling has been repainted green, orange and white, and all our furniture is pushed up against the walls. In the middle of the room Auntie Eileen is sitting on a grey velvet cushion. Behind her, on the beige settee, sits Uncle Michael. Uncle Michael is wearing a rose-patterned shirt that smells of rotten marzipan and stale sponge cake.

"What's up? What's happening?" we ask. "Where's Gaynor's dad?" Nobody answers. Uncle Seamus walks out from the kitchen carrying a yellow notebook marked "TOP SECRET." He looks up at us. So do Auntie Eileen and Uncle Michael, and in that moment we realize something horrible must have happened. Their eyeballs have all gone white. Cecil screams, stretching my mouth, and just then there's a loud knock at our front door.

"Patrick? Patrick, are you in there?" It's Auntie Jude, speaking my dad's real name through the half-open letterbox. "Patrick? Let me in, for God's sake."

Keeping Mum

Kev

The cottage is dark. It's eerily silent, except for the sound of men stirring in their sleep. In the kitchen a murmuring radio, one man listening, and the remains of last night's dinner – roast goose, infinitely better than Arctic-ration compo – festering away in the pedal bin where it was deposited: giblets, skin, grease and purplish bones.

Defending British soil is something I'm used to: when I was a child I spent whole afternoons on Blackpool Pleasure Beach defending England from the Irish Sea. I'd dig myself a trench and stand inside it, dig it deeper until it became a moat. With the sand I'd shifted I would build an enormous castle, crenellate it with hard-packed, upturned plastic buckets of the stuff, then stick in a ragged seagull's feather as Union Jack. I would then enjoy fifteen minutes, at most, of absolute mastery, before my younger sister Angie came running over the sand in her frilly swimming costume, begging to be allowed to join my side. That's what she would call it, my "side." Back on the beach my parents would be standing right behind her, Dad with his trousers rolled up exposing his knees, Mum in a blue flowery smock matching her varicose veins. *Go on*, Dad would mouth. *Go on. Do it.* So of course I did, pulling her up with one arm, trying to ignore her untrimmed toenails digging into the tops of my feet and then officially appointing her my leftwing defence, an aggravating crab clinging to my back as the tide slowly crept in and surrounded us, filled our moat and inevitably climbed up its walls.

The snot constantly caked around her nostrils. The nylon dresses caught in the crack of her arse: the older she got, the more disgusting she seemed to me. I never wanted her to die, exactly. Just to bugger off. It was bad enough having terrible acne. The last possible thing I ever needed was a big fat Mongol on my "side." Sometimes I see her tucked up in my old bed, snoring her face off, blissfully ignorant, or playing "mother," putting fifteen sugars, because I asked her to, into my tea. Sappy scenes that jump out fast like monsters on a bloody ghost-train ride, whenever I let my mind slide back to that time. Eight years since I was last in Blackpool. Meanwhile I'm a Para, and proud of it. Big fat Angie is dead. These the facts I find myself recounting, in what passes for a bed here in the South Atlantic, wondering if I'll leave this tour alive.

Vi

Angie was an odd-looking baby, wrinkled and cone-headed. Not surprising, really: it had taken six hours to push her out. Afterwards – the ugly hole in Harold's head almost forgotten, my great cervix shrinking back – I felt nothing but a numb sort of relief. From now on life would be a simple matter of manipulating objects: stuffing baby arms and legs into babygro's, chopping vegetables for a Lancashire hotpot; all basic outlines remaining intact.

Yet I wasn't shocked when we got the news. I didn't really react at all. Life was just too busy. My reaction came later. One day I was clearing out the garage and came across Kevin's bucket and spade. We hadn't been to Blackpool since the year after Angie was born, I don't know why really. Anyway, I got them out for her to play with. It was a nice spring day. We sat in the garden and I tried showing her how to dig up soil, "Come on, make a sandcastle for Mummy," but she didn't get it. The little blue spade kept slipping out of her grasp. Suddenly, without me even realizing, my arm lashed out as if it had a mind of its own – "Come on, make a sandcastle for Mummy" – and she was bleeding. I'd scratched her with one of my nails, just below her left eye. "Oh my God," I said, and took her in my arms, prising her hand away from the cut. "I can't do this," I said, but there was no one to hear me. Only Angie and God, and I no longer prayed.

Kev

Naa, I'm not worried. The last thing a Para wants to get is soft. And I'm not like these other blasé old bastards – Griffiths, Peacock and the like. I could pretend it doesn't turn my crank, the thought of seeing action – finally! – but the truth is I'm totally fucking pumped.

Fortunately it happens quickly. Most of our whirlybirds are down, courtesy of the Argies, so the only way up to the front is to walk. Eighty-odd miles. Before darkness falls, we set off running. The fucking Marines, like the big girls' blouses they are, yomp the distance with all their home comforts in tow. We travel light, weapons and webbing only. The bergens catch up to us every couple of days. Meanwhile drinking peat water, even sterilized, gives us the most spectacular diarrhea. They don't tell you that in the recruiting posters: *Join the Army and the world will fall out of your bottom.* Some of us stop wearing underpants altogether. Cuddling up to Peacock the second night for warmth I try not to notice the stink.

It's hard to know what's worse, finding your moustache frozen solid to a poncho, going to bed with the squits then waking up with them or living in fear of losing an extremity to trench foot. Some of the lads can hardly walk on the third day because of blisters. O'Toole for example. All he can bloody talk about are socks: dry socks, wet socks, Argie socks, British socks, and how in the Great War the best men continued to move forward even on rotten, useless stumps. The poor fart winces with every step, but the only way out for him's by casevac, and who the hell's going to do that because of foot rot? Not when the day after tomorrow's our big day.

Vi

When the news comes, it's already light out. The clock beside our bed says a quarter past four. The landlady Doris's knock is tentative at first, but quickly gets louder. In the end it's Harold who gets up, pulls a towel around him and answers the door.

The last time Harold and I heard hide nor hair was over a year ago. He was phoning from a pub. I could hardly hear him speak for the noise – glass smashing, vandalists swearing, some of them in foreign tongues – he was drunk of course, three sheets to the wind. It was closing time. He wished us Happy Christmas and said he'd be home to visit in the New Year, but he never was. I wanted to get his number, somewhere to call him back, but he rang off. I spent that Christmas Day in floods of tears. Harold had bought me a lovely bottle of perfume, *Roses, Roses*, by Avon, but I couldn't bear the stink of it, how like the smell of roses it actually was. We've always had yellow roses, climbers, growing in summer around our front door. Mind you, I perked up later. A couple of glasses of sherry for medicinal purposes, and a stiff round of Scrabble – Harold fitted TRANSLATE onto my DEBIT's T and got himself a fifty point bonus – ended up being just the ticket. Still, later that day I finally took the photograph of him in his uniform, ceremonial dress, looking so pink and young, off the living room mantelpiece. I just couldn't stand looking at it any longer, thinking about how much he'd made us suffer, all our hopes smashed to smithereens.

I can tell by the way she whispers that Doris feels guilty. After she leaves Harold leans against the doorframe and lets out a sigh, a deep one, like the exhalation of a submarine going down. When we first met, Harold was beautiful, unconscious. I was the one who was supposed to be innocent, hopeful.

"Violet," he murmurs, "Violet," and shakes me gently. For one brief second I pretend to sleep. Then I switch on the lamp.

Kev

Finally we get to La Casa Blanca, our name for the farmhouse settlement we'll be using as base camp. It's one big, white-washed house, a few barns and half a dozen outbuildings. O'Toole says it reminds him of his great-aunt's croft in Galway. While the officers set up in there, us Toms are sent off to dig in. It's fucking freezing up here. Minus fifteen, endless sucking peat bogs, nothing to see in the distance but rock, rock, more rock and the occasional sleet or snowfall just to keep things festive. Griffiths whistles Christmas carols while his teeth chatter. The earth's so solid our shovels bounce back when they hit the ground. No one knows how long we'll have to stay here. The other lads head off on recce patrols. Meanwhile we make ourselves cozy, as cozy as possible. Any fool can be uncomfortable.

We rest there for 24 hours then get our orders. D-day is to be the 11th of June – tomorrow. It's then I begin to wonder if I can really hack it. Advance to contact across a barren ridge potentially in full view of the enemy – a dream op, surely, for a man who desires to find himself dick-deep in serious action. Only just then I wonder if that man is really me.

That night we're marched across the mountainside to the start-line, sweating despite the sleet under the weight of ammo, grenades, bullets and magazines, rifle and bayonet. The moon casts a metallic light over everything. At the start-line, on the other side of a river, the CO instructs us to attach our bayonets. "What would we want to do that for?" asks Griffiths, always the wisecracker. Peacock's face glistens with tears. For some reason I find myself thinking of the old man, wounded in action, how that Hun grenade got him evacuated, and could conceivably be blamed for my standing right here. And this is how we advance, shivering, into enemy territory, H-hour 0013 hours, Zulu time.

Crawl forward through moonlight, watch nothing happen. Crawl forward some more. Still nothing happens. Then the sound, far-off in 3 Platoon territory, of a landmine exploding. Who the fucking hell got it? No time to wonder. Suddenly we're facing pup tents, a ragged huddle of them. A long in-held breath of hesitation follows, and then the battle begins.

Harold
The doctor, when we finally get to see him, is an Indian chappie. He tells us there's a fifty percent chance our son will live. I tell him that's not good enough, there's got to be a greater chance our Kevin will pull through than that of a coin landing on heads as opposed to tails, but he tells me there isn't. Dr. Chowdhury, I tell him, this woman here brought me back to life when I was a vegetable, and that was in '44 before they had ultrasound, before they had X-rays practically. Are you telling me we can put men on the moon and

wipe out Russia with one push of a secret button and there's nothing you can do to save our Kev?

We're doing everything we can, says Dr. Chowdhury. And of course he is, I mean of course they all are, I say, but we can't lose another one.

Vi is sitting beside our boy, holding his hand.

Kevin is hooked up to machines that do all the things we think life should do for us like breathing, keeping the heart pumping. He's thin and bruised and already there are white hairs poking out between the brown ones on his head. I look at the blood that's dried around the IV needle in his arm.

"That's my blood, that is," I say, without even thinking. "Type O. O for ordinary." Violet sniffs loudly. At least that's some reaction. "Chin up, love. The doctor says there's a good chance he might live."

That's what they said to us about Angela. They said there was a good chance she'd make it to adulthood, provided she took her tablets and got regular check-ups. Well, sixteen isn't adult, not in my book. They also said she was only mildly retarded – mild to moderate retardation, I think the doctor said. The week before she died I found her wandering about the back garden in her nightdress at three in the afternoon with cuts on her feet from walking on broken glass. She said she thought it was stardust. I'd taught her the word not long before, after we'd heard someone saying it on the radio.

The day she died I stood over her, not knowing whether to administer First Aid or not, or if so, how. I knew it was my duty as a father but something in me told me to just let her go.

"Is that what you've been mad at me about all these years?" I ask Violet suddenly, already knowing the answer. After standing with my mouth hanging open watching my daughter die for several seconds I became aware that day of Violet my wife staring at me. She was standing behind me horrorstruck at the top of the stairs. I remember she had a dishtowel in her hands, a faded brown one, *Greetings from the Isle of Wight*. She'd only been standing there for less than a moment, but it was long enough for her to memorize my features, to be able to pick me out of a police lineup when the moment came. Yes I was guilty. As I turned to look at her she pushed past me, threw herself down on top of Angie and began doing chest compressions and the kiss of life, and at that I came to, unfroze and ran downstairs to call an ambulance all the while knowing we were too late.

"You think I wanted her to die, don't you?" I say, the knuckles of my fists turning yellowish-white like dead flesh in the heat of my lap. "You think I did nothing."

Vi's face is tighter than a furled chrysanthemum. People always buy you them or lilies. I hate the look of cut flowers wrapped in cellophane, like birds trapped frantic inside a house.

Kev

They're firing on us from all sides. They're all across the ridge and we're firing back and it's run like hell can hardly breathe shit the fucking safety pin on the hand grenade won't come out have to stand on it to pull it out. Got it out. Someone's down I can see them bouncing down the ridge, a body bouncing off rocks don't know who it is can't look afraid to look Jesus there's another a Tom jerking spasming. It's sweat and cold and noise, flashes, my feet, God how much further to that bunker. The bunker. The enemy. We post in grenades then it's us over the bloody top sandbags bayonet pointed stick the bayonet into the eye left eye turn and pull pull it out suck of resistance lift up onto the next one the cunts the fucking cunts the fucking Argie bastards stick it to them they're all down two surrender sixteen seventeen years old maybe CO screams at us move on we move on under cover small arms fire to a rocky outcrop the next shelter. I'm shaking. Christ I have to shit so badly. Slide off the webbing drop the trousers squat do the business finish suddenly a flash blind I'm on my back shit in my face legs tangled in webbing God did they get me no pain miracle I turn my head see Peacock down his combats ripped wet moaning the bastard's moaning. I crawl over. Blood spurts out of his chest when I press against him. Jesus Christ his heart I can see his heart spinal cord ribcage splinters of bone flapping denim. All right, Cocksy, I tell him, you're all right, we'll get you sorted, but it's too late his eyes have glazed over heart not twitching retch of death in his throat. Then a hand grabs me from behind lifts me up it's O'Toole, leave him, he says, leave him, Grigson, we'll come back. But I can't forget am suddenly seeing again for the first time the way she looked so shocked angry almost as if someone had tricked her stolen her half of a Mars bar or ripped the mini-dress off one of her Sindy dolls. The way she looked at me, as if I'd done it, which in a sense I had, telling her the pills were actually poison, which they were of course, in the right dose, for any normal person, but not for her, no, they were keeping her alive. That pile of sticky saliva-melted tablets all joined together like the droppings of some psycho rabbit underneath the beech hedge beside our house, exactly where I'd told her, so she must have been spitting them out there for several days. I can't forget, even though I'd give my life to, the way Cocksy looked at me before he died, grinning stupidly as if the hole in his chest was some kind of stunt he was pulling, a joke that I was too fucking dense to get.

By the time O'Toole finds me, I've cracked into two separate people one of whom is crapping his nonexistent underpants while the other isn't because he's back there with Peacock already stone cold useless. We run on: fifteen minutes of agony, under heavy artillery fire to the next enemy bunker. I'm vomiting bile and water every three or so minutes. It's kill or be killed: three more seventeen-year-old Argentinian privates to bayonet before breakfast. I'm losing my touch, my mind, miss one's eye and end up spearing him in the left cheek, almost ripping his mouth off. But those stalwarts, O'Toole and Griffiths, covered in blood and filth, are right there beside me. I can't let them see me losing it. Then just as we're moving off one poor bastard grabs me, I feel his hand close tight around my boot and look down. His other hand is on a crucifix. He's pleading with me, something something something por favor, but I don't speak Spanish. What the fuck is he asking? Jesus Christ, the man's desperate, pleading with me. I'm about to reach down and touch him when Griffiths produces his pistol and shoots the man square through the side of the head. The man's grey brains spill out, and I notice his ears are missing. Then he morphs into Angie. Someone cut off my poor dead sister's ears.

Harold

They've given us a list of Kevin's personal effects: T-shirt, cagoule, denim jeans, socks, underpants, trainers, gentleman's watch (broken), handkerchief and comb. Childproof plastic pill vial containing 450 mg Desyrel (50 mg tablets). Leatherette wallet containing Midlands bank card, ticket stub for *An Officer and a Gentleman*, worn Polaroid photograph of a girl and boy eating ice cream (Kev and Angie back in '65), scrap of paper with word "ears" scribbled across it, £20 and 58 pence in bills and change.

The gun was his, it was in his hands, and the fingerprints on it were his also. The only strange thing was that he had missed. Normally blokes shoot themselves through the mouth – we've all seen it, on TV and so forth – but Kevin tried to shoot himself in the heart. Fortunately he didn't manage it. The bullet missed by less than an eighth of an inch.

He was at the cinema. He was taking antidepressants. He has a bank account. He was carrying a picture of him and Angie around, one I took of them on the Pleasure Beach, back in happier days. All these objects tell me something about him, something about the son I thought I knew.

The one thing I don't understand are these "ears." What ears is he talking about? Why did he have that written down, and in his pocket? Is it short for something, code for something, some kind of drugs maybe, Lord knows what he's been getting himself into. I just think if I could only understand it maybe we could get through to him, lying there. They say if he wakes up then maybe he'll make it.

"Your missus has gone for a coffee. Can I get you anything?" asks the nurse.

"No, thanks, love."

"How did that happen, Mr. Grigson?" she asks, touching my scar lightly with her fingertips.

"Oh, in the War," I answer. As if it wasn't obvious. "Just like what happened to him." I go over to my son and bend down next to his ear. It's pale and waxy. "I know you're in there," I whisper.

The girl who called Doris was Kevin's downstairs neighbour, not a girlfriend or a lover as I'd foolishly hoped. She seemed a good sort, the kind of lass you'd like to see only your son wed: bonny and kind but with her wits about her. Before she left, she took my hand in hers and gave me a look that said, "I know you're in there." She knew this strange weeping man wasn't all I was.

Kev

The battle has petered out. I assume we've won. One of the other platoons is marching on Stanley, but we stay where we are, keep an eye on the prisoners. Griffiths and some of the others centralize the dead – check dog-tags, remove all weaponry and ammunition, assemble bodies for collection. I'm told to be at ease. The stench of blood, cordite, and morphine is overwhelming. O'Toole has shrapnel in his calf, and Sandiford has lost his left leg altogether. The Doc is wrapping his shredded stump in a desperate tourniquet, meanwhile he lies silent, dosed up on morphine. There are tears coursing down my cheeks.

I don't know if I am alive anymore, or if I'm one of those bags of canvas filled with blood and bone fragments they're calling brave: ex-men, dead men, sentimental bags of meat to be buried half-frozen in some corner of a foreign land that will forever be Argentina. It's no surprise when I stumble across a corporal skewered on a bayonet several yards away, his eyes still open. One of ours. I decide to strip him, find in his munitions pouch a collection of flesh stubs: earlobes, slippery as burned out candles. I count up seventeen.

"What about these, Sir?"

"Good God, Grigson, where the hell did you find – put them with the rest of them, I mean the enemy dead. And don't say a word to anyone, do you hear?"

"No, Sir."

I can't hear any more because some poor bastard is screaming, moaning, perhaps it's Sandiford. Then the CO orders me to go with the wounded. I have a superficial bullet scratch but that's not it. They know I've seen something.

They want to get me out of here in case I squeal. Except I already am.

We're flown out by helicopter to the field hospital, and then from there to the hospital ship, where they put me in the psychiatric area. It all happens so damn quickly, I don't have time to tell them about their mistake. On board the beds are full of men whose faces resemble the remains of fires left in grates, unrecognizable and caked with ash. Sometimes the swollen slit of an eye half-opens, or a bubble emerges from the melted stub of a nose. Their faces, hands and arms are stiff and statue-like, encased in bandages or plastic bags. I wander between them when left alone, looking for the enemy prisoner whose ears were taken, but I can't find her. There's a tag round my neck and they've left me my ampoule of morphine, standard issue for all of us sods in case of injury. I unscrew the cap and jab the needle as close as possible toward my heart.

"Think of it as extra-strong heroin," says the medic when I surface from the infinite waves of blackness. "You're not going to die but you will have a damn good trip." He pats my knee, a disgusted expression on his face, like I'm some kind of urine-stained dosser. Then he moves away and talks in a low voice to some of the nurses. They don't leave me alone ever after that.

It's grey and muggy, summer, when we get back to Blighty. The sky presses down like bloodstained gauze. They send me directly to the Army hospital psychiatric wing where I don't sleep a wink for five and a half weeks. The pictures they transmit into my brain, the severed earlobes of my brother Argies, of my sister Angie, the heart medicine spat out between rounds of shells are all designed to confuse me, make me forget what I saw there but I never will.

"Well done, son," says my dad, not looking at me. "We showed them, didn't we? I mean you did. I heard it was cold out there. It takes a bit of time to get over these things but you will, son, you will. Just remember we're proud of you. Your mother and I, we're just so —" then his voice breaks and he has to clear his throat.

"Lovely view," says Mum. "Look at all those lovely rose bushes. Can you go for a walk yet? I've brought you a couple of magazines to read." Two copies of *Family Circle*.

After that they run out of things to say, sit and fidget, then catch the train back up north.

Eventually the officers find a sleeping pill strong enough to keep me under for a couple of days, and I start to feel less certain they want to break me. No one seems interested in what I have to say, or at least do their best not to react. I can't tell them about the words I'm hearing, unrepeatable and unpronounceable, spoken by someone just to the left of my head. I know it's a collaboration with the enemy to get me locked away for the rest of my life, some sort of tape recording of swear-words in Spanish, and if I admit to hearing them I'm sunk, so I just keep mum.

"We're giving you a clean bill of health," says the doc, one fine morning in August. "You're free to go. Would you like to phone your parents?"

"No, thanks," I say. "I think I'd rather surprise them," which I do, by phoning from a service station halfway up the M6 and telling them I was responsible for Angie's death.

They refuse to believe me.

"Well, fuck you," I say. "Fuck you both," and walk back out to the road.

Vi

When your future husband is lying helpless beneath you, his personality fractured by the weapons of our country's deadliest enemy, you have to feel a little gratitude. After all, how else would you ever have found him? You put him back together piece by piece, and the bit that's missing, the bit that was there in all that mud and filth killing men and fighting for its survival you just allow to disappear. And when he touches you next, takes your hand and leads it to his head, you let go and reach in further down.

Life is what matters. The life your daughter has, making up jigsaws, fitting the cardboard tabs into their slots with such deep satisfaction she doesn't even notice there are no more.

Life is what you are feeding to your son now, in level teaspoons. You are no longer the breast to which he's attached, but his mouth is wet again, hungry, open and speechless. You can at least fill it. You can do that much.

Kev

I spent a month living under a bridge. At least it was dry under there, although I was sharing my patch beside the skip with several rats and one other crazy old codger who called himself Bitsy, a toothless 30-year-old schizophrenic who would sing tenor arias to the seagulls in between swigs of turpentine and fits of trembling, spitting paranoia. I spent several weeks working illegally on a building site with a bunch of blokes from Poland, one of whom tried to get me to marry his sister. I was taken to the loony bin one freezing December night after a copper fished me out of the Manchester Ship Canal in which I'd been attempting to drown. They gave me sedatives and anti-psychotics but all I really wanted was some blow. Only when I was stoned did the voice that still talked to me speak clearly, allowing me to translate what it said.

I got out of there by lying, by telling them I never saw or heard anything unusual and that I was only sad because I'd lost my job. The fact was I didn't really have a job. I'd been living hand to mouth, a bit of begging, a bit of shoplifting, the odd day or two of cash in hand. Every now and then I thought of my parents, celebrating my dead sister's birthday each year with a cake covered in candles, as if she were still wheezing, still alive. Very rarely did I think of Angie. But when I did it was mostly out of jealousy, that she was gone and I was still bloody here. Did I really do her a favour? Did I do Cocksy a favour, leaving him to die out on that field rather than giving him the chance to be patched up by butchers and shipped home to face life on the dole?

Eventually I ended up in Runcorn, driving cabs and drinking too much, living in a flat that used to belong to my mate Luke. For a few precious weeks I thought I'd done it, thought I'd outrun the demons and found, if not a home, then at least a place I could rest for a few breaths. I put up posters, bought myself some brand new trainers, the new U2 album, the gun I'd been carrying around, a 9mm, away in a cupboard, telling myself I wouldn't need it, not in this neck of the woods. I'd acquired it from a mate, also ex-Army, who'd served down south as well, and was now running a betting shop in Hull. He used to hunt and was totally obsessed with firearms. I told him I'd made some enemies; he didn't ask questions, didn't know they were the kind no one else can see.

Most of my fares were prostitutes. I didn't mind them. I worked all night and slept most of the day. One afternoon I was emptying my rubbish and ran into the girl who lived downstairs. What I noticed first were her fingers, long, slim and bare, almost shameful. I wanted to touch them but mine were covered in dirt.

After that I looked for her every day, got to know her routine, how she'd come home at exactly 5:15 then go out again for a walk or down the shops. One Saturday I went up to her door, determined to knock and invite her out for a drink –

she didn't seem to have a boyfriend – when it occurred to me that this all might be a trap, an elaborate trap to get me to confess to what I'd done, or come to believe now that I must have, that I was the one who had chopped off all the ears. They'd been tracking me all this time and now this was the ultimate test, the bait I was expected to fall for. For although I had no idea how I'd done it, what tools I'd used or how I put the pieces in that bag, it seemed obvious now, as it had for some time, that this was the real reason I was evacuated, the real reason they'd invalided me out, left me with a record no one would wish for, the stain of cowardice, of psychological defeat. I was the monster who'd mutilated those corpses, I was the boy who'd persuaded my sister to die.

I never asked her out. Instead I stopped working and stayed home. Drinking, smoking. Trying to persuade the Spanish voice to accuse me, to finally confess in plain English what it was I'd done. Por favor, I begged, grabbing at its trousers. My heart was hanging out, my spine was showing, I was all alone on an island, the tide rising quickly, and soon its sandy peak would be submerged.

Then, at the eleventh hour, the girl saved me. It was all so simple. She came upstairs and knocked on my door, which I answered, but only opened a crack. Behind me the place was strewn with cans and bottles. Her ears were like the soft insides of shells.

"Are you all right?"

"Yes, yes, I'm fine, thank you."

"Only I heard shouting. And you haven't picked up your milk for five days."

"No, no, everything's fine."

"I'm Molly, by the way."

"Kevin."

"Nice to meet you. Well, I'll leave you to yourself, then."

"Thanks."

"Okay, bye."

After I'd heard her go back in downstairs I decided to go out and get some air. I pulled on my cagoule and trainers, stuffed some cash in my pocket and left the house.

It was a beautiful night, cold, but not as cold as I'd expected. I walked for hours, passing a cinema outside of which I picked up a ticket stub for a film that was playing, imagining it was some kind of message. I found a scribbled note stuck in my pocket, and a snapshot of me and Angie at Blackpool. A woman in a red ski jacket passed me, calling my name. The world was talking to me and not in Spanish. I thought perhaps it had finally joined my side.

But when I got back to my flat he was waiting for me, the young Argentinian with the girlish eyes. He'd found my pistol. I didn't beg for mercy but felt glad he'd found me, unzipped my cagoule and showed him my heart.

"There, my friend, that is where you need to shoot me."

I didn't hear a thing when the shot was fired, although I did watch the bullet glide out toward me, caught it between my ribs here, a perfect own goal. Instantly the voice stopped talking, the one that's been lodged by my head for the past three years.

Vi

There's always a moment in which rescue's possible; I was trained to seize it. Even in the Army hospital, surrounded by the mute and the incompetent, I threw my rope down into the well, dug deep into the airless snow bank, crawled on hands and knees through the burning house. I've removed shrapnel fragments from inside a human liver, rescued a gold chain dropped down a stinking sewer, even shoved my fist up the back end of a cow in order to untangle the cord of a crowning calf.

I'm beside my boy's bed, willing him to come to, and, more than that, to know who I am. Through the scrim of my exhaustion I watch him, buried up to his neck in toothpaste green, will him to begin thrashing and writhing, to try at least to articulate the damage, the hole in his chest, the collapsed right lung, the floating rib fragments, the opening in his back where the bullet came out, taking a piece of intercostal muscle with it, on its journey into the plaster and lath of his living room wall.

"Kevin," I say, "Kevin, don't be a baby," even though he *is* in fact an infant, an infant who holds inside it the mind of a man. "Kevin, I'm your mother. Can't you see me? Don't you recognize me? Kevin! Come on, sunshine, squeeze my hand."

His hand, twice the size of mine, remains limp. Over the last ten days it seems to have grown thin and yet puffy, to have turned, in fact, into the hand of a very old man.

What if Harold had ended up like this?

I take a break, go for another walk down hospital corridors, lose myself in the squeak of nurses' shoes, rubber wheelchair tires, the shuffle of paper slippers, birth certificates. Go as far as I can before turning back. Then instead of heading for Kev's ward, turn sharp left.

In the waiting room I sit down opposite my husband. Across the little coffee table, between a small pile of books and a half-empty Tupperware container of egg salad sandwiches, I reach for his hand, place mine on top of it. How rough a gentleman's skin is, cracked and even raw sometimes, in places. "Harold," I say, out loud, without even thinking about it, "Harold, I know I've asked you this before, but how did it feel in the War, when you shot a German?"

"Well, my love," he replies, his eyes shining, "Well." He pauses. "It didn't feel like much, to be perfectly honest. Although …" Instead of finishing his sentence he reaches for the back of his head, dips his fingers into the gap his scar scoops out, and examines them closely. I feel left out, start to examine my own frosted ovals, as if the rest of his story were stuck to their ends.

"Mr and Mrs Grigson?" All of a sudden a nurse we haven't seen before pokes her streaked-blonde head around the waiting-room door. "Sorry to interrupt, but there's been a development."

"Well, Harold," I say. We head for the corridor.

Our son is sitting upright. His eyes are open. We walk toward him in wonderment, barely breathing, the rip in what's normal suddenly visible, an opening the size of a hand grenade – which is to say, the size of a human heart.

Going to India

ALL THE GUIDEBOOKS splayed across her dresser do not protect Jackie from being mugged. In between feedings, she is strangled. Then, while the sun sets copper over the Hooghly, her attacker frisks her body for drugs. Now that she's dead there'll be no one left for him to make fun of. They'd only been lovers for three weeks, but it was okay. Jackie has nice hair, but now even her spiral perm is matted, black blood smeared across her mouth.

Kolkata fizzles. Jackie's body fragments, pieces of it unrecoverable, while three-month-old Brody clamps down on her left nipple and sucks. This must be the twelfth nursing since bedtime. And this time, after he's finished, he bites.

Jackie clutches her tit. Brody's two teeth sink even deeper; she sticks her finger in; his wet mouth smears her as he unpops. For a moment she drifts, corpselike, through an eerie silence. Then Brody bellows again and Jackie jumps up.

His screams are eating tunnels through her brain tissue. His neck is hot, her hands close tight. Between her fingers, small bones grate against each other. For a moment she lets go and then, calm and decisive, grabs him by the shoulders and hurls him across the pitted futon. He lands on his face. Jackie watches him flail. He's only just learned to roll over. As he gathers momentum, approaches his tipping point, she wonders if he will suffocate this time.

It's 4:12 a.m. in Vancouver, 3:42 p.m. back in Kolkata. Half a day ahead, her waterlogged corpse decomposes, maggot lilies rooting through its eyes: when her lover comes to he will be distraught, rage against a sea of indifferent faces only to forget her as soon as the ganja takes hold. It doesn't take long for guilt, and the dead, to disintegrate. Jackie herself, shivering on her wrought-iron balcony, disappears too. What's another maternal homicide-suicide? A flake of fall-out drifting down from bleached black sky.

She goes back inside, into the bathroom, takes down her back-up pack of razors. Brody's screams are becoming breathless. The pain as she presses the blade down both explodes her and cools. Going to India has helped her through a bad patch, but now the trick no longer seems to work. The truth is, at 32 she has never been anywhere. Instead, her life arcs out a modest decline: a first job as a waitress that led to several others as a hostess, one year in college, a failed attempt to enter the film industry, several recent excursions through massage parlours. Forced to explain, she'd adopt her mother's analysis. It's a class conspiracy! Days spent fucking the rich as if they were equals, when all along they were plotting her oppression, her death. Questions still plague her: Is it too late to emigrate to New Zealand? What if she accepts Crazy's offer to set her up as a madam in Dubai?

Blood flows, a Middle Eastern river. Brody is fine, although he is still distraught. Soon a neighbour will come, or perhaps a police officer. There must be someone out there who cares. Meanwhile someone is knocking on her door. A rancid towel wrapped around hot breasts, Jackie peers, blinded, into the low-ceiling corridor. The same thing happened last night. Is the complex haunted? A soft, female finger runs up her nape.

That woman Nadia, winding an endless, multicoloured scarf around her neck – hadn't she just come back from Mumbai?

Jackie tries again, this dreams herself into some sort of ashram, the hallway of a big old house in Kitsilano, where women and men take off their shoes and step lightly into a sun-dappled room. Daffodils and crocuses outside near the window, the scent of dhal bhat cooking on a gas stove. Nadia is there, limber and buff. When Jackie finished her one year of General Science, her room in residence was clean and tidy, unlike the others', the travelers', whose laminate boxes were brittle with sacred tack. It felt like it had been that way since the beginning, everyone thoroughly marinated in Nag Champa while she stood watching, ugly and gauche in her sweats.

Carving a shallow X into her forearm, Jackie examines everything except her own body, that black legginged, T-shirted thing with its arms raised she knows is the main reason she cannot relax, because it reconnects her with her history: with Brody, his harelip, blotchy complexion; with Ulrike, her mother.

Nadia's scarf wound round and round the stiff collar of a Nehru jacket; waist-length, honey-blonde hair trapped deep inside.

"So lovely to see you!" Nadia beckons. The scent of curry wound around her fingers, intimately entwined with a whiff of Earl Grey.

Jackie shakes her head. It occurs to Jackie that she must have been attracted. She doesn't usually think of herself that way, but there was something about how the woman touched her, a well-lubricated hand pressed to Jackie's navel, that broke through and registered: her last erotic encounter before childbirth, which was hardly erotic, except for the moment they placed him on her chest. If only she had realized what was happening! Perhaps she would now be employed and in a relationship instead of naked and bloodstained on the lino.

She blinks. Nadia is fading. The ashram is difficult to stabilize, unlike Kolkata, which wouldn't leave. *Kitsilano*, thinks Jackie, pinching her calf muscle, watching herself, a stick woman, felt-tipped and sketchy, tumbling rapidly out of a hasty arm balance, rendered clumsy by Nadia's beauty, her grace.

Her mother cried the day Jackie quit college. This was not unusual. Ever since her husband died Ulrike wept freely, her tears just part of the liquid with which she scrubbed floors. This did not mean she was overemotional. On the contrary; her grasp of brute economics was nuanced and fine.

"Look what happened to Lenin," she would mutter darkly, if anyone smart threatened to succeed. Those five neat piles of old *Unsere Zeiten* still alphabetized and earmarked under Jackie's bed. Ulrike knows nothing about Brody. The last time Jackie visited Kelowna her mother was screaming German at the top of her lungs.

According to Google, the German for cloth diaper is *Windeln*. Brody wears Life brand disposables, their waistbands decorated with teddies and rattles. After he was born, Jackie once shat her own pants, running for the telephone. A third-degree tear and postpartum depression had seemed a small price to pay, then, for becoming human, which was what she thought raising him would eventually involve.

Now she's not sure. She blots the blood off. Why is she so afraid of going back in? His tiny fists, mottled with frustration. Her mother's bad chest, rattling through the Okanagan winters. Ulrike has never told her anything, not even how she came to Canada. Everything cobbled together from rumours, snippets of conversation overhead at meetings, where they went weekly until Jackie was nine. Was it the CCF or the Socialist Workers? Brody has no language, no distinguishing features, yet his face still means more to Jackie than Trotsky's, or Christ's.

Six weeks after dropping out of college, Jackie found herself back in Kelowna where Ulrike cooked up schnitzel and railed against capitalism, already forgetting what day it was, what ring she'd left on. Ulrike was not sympathetic. Instead she cleared her throat and announced that Jackie should stop being selfish, help someone less fortunate than herself. "Travel to India, Africa, teach revolution. That is what will cure you of this weakness." Ulrike Bachmann, her crazy mother, white-haired, baton thin, jabbing her finger at a ripped-apart map, its white-edged flaps tectonic plates shifting. Her mother's brief marriage to a used furniture salesman named Ellison the only good thing she has ever admitted happening. Ellison died when Jackie was five. His marriage to Ulrike lasted eleven months.

"Technically, I'm dead, too," whispers Jackie, dropping the razor, "murdered in a dream about traveling to India." Is that what she'll say from her straitjacket, when they come?

The glowing skin she associates with a clear conscience was what attracted Jackie to Brody's dad. They met at a party where everyone else was married. Tanked up on coolers, she slammed into him again in an upscale tapas bar where he was celebrating his recent divorce. His graying hair a shock above smooth, brown cheekbones, his physique that of an avid mountain climber, Jackie thought she had landed feet-first when he asked for her number, only to discover, later, that she had not. Far from rich, Prince Charming was unemployed, unstable, bipolar. She should have known. Closing the door of her apartment behind his sister, who had dropped by one evening to tell her the truth, Jackie sighed but secretly felt relieved. She and Luc had slept together four times. She had found his patter impressive, if slightly unnerving. About to chalk it up, she discovered the worst.

The test strip still wet, her old friend Sarah-Jane suggested abortion. After all, Jackie was single, on antidepressants and hadn't had a stable job for weeks. Her unfinished degree was a sinister joke. She no longer mentioned it.

"I can't." As Jackie watched her red wine swirl down Sarah-Jane's sink she knew they wouldn't be seeing much more of each other. From now on it would be sobriety, vegetables and B vitamins, creating some kind of nursery in the bedroom where a picture of her mother at eighteen hung on the wall.

The temp job held on long enough for her to get mat leave, and going cold turkey was easier than she'd expected, perhaps because the symptoms matched. Jackie tried not to think about the damage: the hip-flask she had drained secretly, daily, up until that Saturday night in week twelve when Sarah-Jane had abandoned her to her fate.

When Brody was born Jackie was alone at the hospital. Attempting to stand, an hour or two later, her insides felt as if they were sliding out, all she had worked so hard to hide splooshing forth uncontrollably onto white lino, a finite, twisted mass of biological material. Her body felt huge and empty, as though she had just given birth to Mars.

"Are you okay, dear?"

The stroller parked a foot away, closed up on itself, the two halves of its waterproof hood almost meeting so no one can see Brody's raw, new face, his tiny nostrils flaring with each in-breath as he swims up close to the surface of sleep and then dives, Jackie looks up. The woman, her interrogator, has dark brown whiskers. She clicks her tongue disapprovingly, plum blossom petals dotting her red wool coat like the corpses of fairies. Is this a dream?

Once upon a time, Jackie presumes, her mother also wanted to be someone. She, too, followed the steps, sat the exams, researched, emigrated, networked and upgraded but none of it worked and now she is two again, screaming for Mutti, strapped to a waterproof mattress, unable to think. Delicate, fashionable Ulrike, whose two blonde braids are trained into perfect ear muffs, staring down from the bedroom wall at Brody as if to say, hey buddy, you and me both. Jackie does not know her father, but if she did she would call him up right now, ask him why he bothered procreating. Does he even know? All Ulrike had said was that he was Canadian and that she had met him in the dome car deep in Saskatchewan and said goodbye somewhere after Banff. For all Jackie knows, Brody is related to half of Moose Jaw. Perhaps she should have him FedExed there. Someone would probably recognize his Slavic features, claim him as their own and then she would be free to return to hooking, that stubborn fifteen pounds notwithstanding. Not that she has turned a trick in years, or ever did. The men she met in bars and accompanied to hotels, the sad, twitchy salesmen with names like Rick and Chuck who emptied their verb-like selves into her passive noun-ness before rolling off their white beds to take a slash, were more like cute collectibles than paying clients, faces she was auditioning for their suitability as Ulrike's well-scrubbed, Prairie counterpart. None of them fit. She made a few bucks and then decided to quit before she became addicted to anything serious. Enter the temp jobs. But now somehow the imprint of their bodies, their bony loins, hairy shoulders and mole-speckled butts have found their way into her as regret, a frail toxin that eats away at her brain cells in much the same way that Ecstasy might.

After her emigration in the mid-fifties Ulrike wanted to leave Germany behind. This is what Ulrike's best friend,

Sabine, said. Not because she had committed any war crimes. Far from it: Ulrike and her brothers actively resisted National Socialism. No, insisted Sabine, chuckling hoarsely, even at eleven, twelve, Ulrike wasn't fooled. But when Dresden was bombed, Ulrike's parents and brother, Peter, perished; another brother later died in combat. What reason did she have to return? Sabine, purple-rinsed and addicted to marzipan, is utterly convinced of Ulrike's heroism. Yet a strange conviction still lingers in Jackie's bone marrow: Ulrike is guilty. Aren't all Germans? Even those whose relatives were crushed by rocks?

Three short taps, and then one last one. This time Jackie leaps up from the floor and undoes the deadbolt just in time to see a hooded figure run down the hallway and out the fire exit.

"Stop!" She yells but it's too late. The door has slammed and now there is nothing again but beige carpet, a small pink object lying inside it, nested into the pile, almost invisible. Jackie picks it up: a plastic bead.

Once, when Jackie was fourteen, Ulrike collapsed in the mall. It was very embarrassing. People walked past, pretending not to see. Get up, Mom, hissed Jackie, catching sight of herself in the liquor store window. Her reflection grimaced. Ulrike stayed on her knees, the toes of her snow boots angling inward like those of a child or someone else innocent kneeling down to pick up what has been dropped.

"Die Frauenkirche!" A cathedral, long since destroyed. Her mother remained on her knees for twenty-five minutes while Jackie paced and shrugged and rolled her eyes. Just as the security guard was growing antsy, threatening to call for an ambulance, Ulrike stood up.

"A great pink angel came down and saved me," she explained later, loading up new needles with speckled yarn.

"It was very – beautiful." Now Jackie wishes she had asked more questions. Did the angel speak English? Did it rescue Ulrike's parents and brothers? What was its name?

Jackie places the bead on her coffee table. Overhead, several ex-lovers clink champagne flutes, toast her insanity. Then her body shatters, drifts off into numberless half-lives. Brody's mother falls down, clutches her chest.

"Help me someone, help, I think I'm dying."

Jackie has cut herself on her arms and is bleeding slightly. Her cell phone sits on her desk, a silver capsule. If only she could just reach out. What about the nurse at the clinic? Or Juniper Grierson, the only other lap dancer/mom she knows? Last week they met for cappuccino, juggling breasts and babies on their laps. Juniper's alone, too. But coping. Her child Aaron has a heart condition. Juniper's legs are slim and smooth. Aaron, at two months, wears immaculate button-down shirts.

"Aren't they just adorable?" coos Juniper.

"Aren't they just."

Since Jackie and Brody came home from the hospital, night and day have been replaced by twilight, its ambivalent blue filling each room with sadness, an endless cycle of nursing, changing and then rocking, Brody screaming for five and a half hours at a stretch while Jackie in her sweats stumbles to and fro in the back alley, the wheels of Brody's stroller worn down to crusts.

"Mutti!" screams Jackie, her powerful voice bouncing off the sponged beige walls.

Kolkata stinks. Her body is cross-hatched with tiny scars.

Back in '88, just before the Wall fell, she and Ulrike visited Dresden together. Ulrike refused to look up relatives and instead spent her time shopping for sausage.

For a few months, while she was pregnant, Jackie would do a tour of the city's bookshops, seek out tour guides to Germany and turn them spine inward. It wasn't exactly stealing, more like stalling. Deleting certain realities for a day or two, massaging facts.

"Mutti, Mutti!"

As Jackie reenters the bedroom to check on Brody the dreaming part of her mind separates vertically. Up there on the ceiling, there's a party. The party is noisy and full of theatrical women in vintage dresses, every steep stair boasting an ashtray, Jackie herself hoarse from chain-smoking Camels. Jackie murmurs assent as Nadia rattles on about transformation, the incredible power Indians have to endure.

Jackie feels breathless, fumbles for her puffer. The bed is a mess, stinks of stale milk and vomit; pacifiers crunch underfoot. For a moment she thinks he's alive. But his chest isn't moving. Her beautiful child, so nondescript viewed in this half light, lying motionless, face down on the duvet. On his pudgy, pale arms Jackie can see small bruises. 4:47.

Nadia, Jackie is certain, had visited India. Not only did she sightsee, she met gurus, even saw one manifest a golden lingam. Nadia, beautiful and brilliant, her life so burnished by privilege she cannot see them, see the thousands of ancestors, with rags in their hands.

The job Nadia offered her was in Wardrobe, sewing up costumes for a movie set in the Depression. There's no reason Jackie can't get another, once Brody is bigger and things have settled, but right now that seems so far away and Jackie knows the industry is volatile. If you're not in, you're out, and Nadia is central. Slapping her in the face was a bad idea, but the woman had had the temerity to touch her, and her public, pregnant body had reacted in kind. Nadia had hissed. How rapidly the rich transform themselves. One moment they are casual, endearing, the next they run the world, have hard, lined faces and live up on Mount Olympus where you cannot find them, in palaces of diamonds, pearls and ice.

4:49. Brody shudders. Jackie swoops down on him, eagle-like, lifts him up from the dark, moist bed. His breath is hot, she places her cheek against his and cradles him, gasping, the noose around her neck made of Dresden china. Brody stiffens and bends back. Her son is reaching. He's awake and he needs her to love him. But she cannot breathe.

Child Abuse

"IS RUBY JEALOUS?" A woman wearing five kinds of expensive leather cradles a miniature schnauzer on her lap. The dog shudders. Alanna touches her, cautious, tickles a tiny white spot in the crook of her neck.

"No, I don't think so. But what I am getting is oatmeal."

"Oatmeal?"

"Yes. Ruby finds it repulsive. She wants you to stop giving it to her for breakfast."

The woman blushes. "I can't believe you just said that."

"It's okay. I have no judgment. I'm just passing on what Ruby tells me – oh, and she says there's a ghost: Rudy? Randy?"

"Oh my God! Rodney."

Ruby's ears prick up and Alanna relaxes. For a moment she could almost believe this is real.

Lately her clients have thinned out. She barely minds, especially since she told that Alsatian to stop eating brownies. Its owner, a balding realtor, claimed the pooch was totally addicted and that was what he wanted her to fix. Placing her hand on the dog's chest, Alanna addressed it as she might a recalcitrant toddler: "Hi, bud, how you doing? What's with all the junk?" Within seconds she was missing the top third of her left pinkie. The blood burned an archipelago into the realtor's cargo pants.

Perhaps she was just not meant to work with animals.

Later, sitting in Emerge with a bandage on her finger the size of a Chihuahua, she even confessed to her sister the whole thing was a hoax: she didn't know her own mind, let alone anyone else's.

"But maybe the dog did," said Charlotte.

"That's why he freaked out." It was hard not to slur. The painkillers were kicking in rapidly.

"But what about Ruby? You got her right."

"Her owner had food stains on her shirt and the name 'Randy' just, I don't know, came to me."

"Wow. Detective?"

"I don't know, Char, I just don't know."

Charlotte and Alanna, the Trout twins, are determined to find their places in the grand scheme of things. They have been looking most of their lives. Their mother lived on welfare, courtesy of Uncle Douglas, who doled it out at the going rate, even asking her to "sign in" every two weeks. Douglas drove truck, and the night he hit a moose their lives were shattered. Jay OD'd and was admitted to hospital. The twins were fostered out. Between them, they lived with eight different families before, eventually moving west. Here in Vancouver they share a one-bedroom and do not tell anyone they are related. Except for one or two special girlfriends, of course.

Charlotte works as a masseuse, insists it's legal. Alanna's not so sure, but then her own employment's not exactly traditional and at least they have furniture, the old rotting mattress they picked up from Value Village now an art project, covered in scribbled graffiti, fake knife wounds. Soon they even plan to move to a two-bedroom, or at least above ground, somewhere they can stand up straight. Their mother's place was a wreck, with towels for curtains and homemade plywood furniture. Neither of the girls ever had a wardrobe, or anywhere to keep their stuff other than plastic bags, but there was always food on the table, and music, Jay a would-be Country singer whose long, slim fingers picked out anxious notes. Charlotte used to sing in a girl band, Rockin' Rosin, pop-tinged folk with fiddles, flutes and four-part harmonies, when they lived back east, but now the two of them rarely admit to such follies. Vancouver is the place they will make their names.

"What should we do? Go for a walk?"

Char doesn't start until early evening. Meanwhile it's spring outside and the kids are at recess, swinging on their stomachs and hanging from bars, and Alanna hates the thump of her blood, the way it thunders, trapped, inside the bandage. "Sure, why not."

Out in the park it's the usual scene: frothy fruit trees, tourists feeding French fries to raccoons. Somewhere out near Siwash Rock a woman with short grey hair and a spiked leather jacket carries a miniature cockapoo in a backpack, its cute ears sticking out of a knitted cap.

"Starbarks!" cry the girls.

"We should get that going." Charlotte rolls her eyes towards the concession. "Fancy a latte?"

While her sister pays, Alanna chuckles, recalling their ongoing list of possible start-ups, each one more ridiculous than the last: bonsai'd kids, yoga for rocks, inflatable parking spots that fit in your pocket. Most of them have already been patented, usually by people in L.A. But filter rabbit, mochachillo milk bones: coffee for dogs seems weird, but not *that* weird.

"Possible TV ad," she mock-dictates into her cell phone, "bichon frise sips Chunky Americano. Close-up reveals

Arabica beans interspersed microscopically with beef cubes. Voice over: Come to Starbarks!..."

"Hey, Lal. Meet Dawn." Charlotte is suddenly back, with two lattes and a brand new friend.

Cockapoo Mama lifts a paw. "Hi."

"Hi."

"I hear you're psychic."

Alanna flashes her sister a furious side glance. "No. Not at all. At least, not really. If I was, I'd have ten fingers. As it is, I only have nine and a half."

Charlotte glares back, over-enunciates. "Dawn is looking for a live-in caregiver."

Alanna is confused. The butch has obvious muscles and glows with superfoods.

"For her dog, Mitzi."

"Ah, right."

"I work in the film industry," offers Dawn, running her eyes up and down Alanna's chest. "You know, long hours, brutal schedule. And Mitzi doesn't like to run with the pack. She needs one-on-one time. We're convinced she's gifted."

"Gifted?"

"Yep. She scores pretty high on Canine Intelligence. But she's neurotic. Ideally we'd like someone with a counseling background. Someone who can take her to classes, get her dressed and fed, engage her intellectually while Mom and Pop bring home the bacon."

"Dawn and Rosana live right here." Charlotte points to a massive new condo development. "Up in the penthouse. They're offering *free room and board* plus a generous living allowance. For years."

"Including a probationary period of six to eight weeks. It's up to Mitz, of course. She's the boss."

"Indeed." Alanna sighs, craves Extra Strength Tylenol. Isn't Charlotte straight? What kind of role does she plan to play? And what classes do cockapoos take anyway? Pilates? Square dance? She's about to walk when a voice interrupts. *Don't go.* She turns back to Mitzi. *Take me for a walk along the beach.*

"Anyway, we need to dash, so here's my card." Dawn grins, hands over a chit decorated with gold leaf. *Doggone Productions, Unlimited.*

"Movies for dogs?"

"Yep. Nothing too exciting. Bar the odd cat massacre, of course."

The following Sunday, Alanna and Charlotte move in. The penthouse has a 360 degree view, and from the balcony they pick out their old building.

"It looks like a fudgsicle."

"As seen from Googlearth."

"I thought you were losing your marbles, that day on the seawall. But so far this is a definite improvement."

"Did I tell you, I gave Rick my notice? Told him I was done giving blow jobs. The fat bastard never even blinked."

"Here's to special-needs dogs." They clink mojitos. From up here, at the very peak of chic, Commercial Drive appears slum-like, a boho *favela*. Alanna wonders how they ever coped. Her bandage now replaced by a modest Band-aid, she's seriously considering film school. And, if that doesn't work out, a swerve into counseling, this time wealthy fuck-ups, though, not dogs.

"You could sue him, you know," says Charlotte, drunk. That realtor."

"Really?"

"Call in WCB."

The two of them almost fall right off the balcony, plummet thirty-two floors to untimely deaths.

The next day at six Rosa knocks on the door: a tawny blonde with a freckled neck. So far, Alanna hasn't quite decided who Mitzi takes after. The dog has Rosa's good looks but also exhibits Dawn's steely charm. It's a toss-up. Or is that a throw-up, the word bulimia not quite on any one's lips. For the dog clearly has trouble keeping food down. Yesterday Mitzi vomited eleven times, after every meal plus whenever the phone rang. This, combined with her ADD, social anxiety disorder and tendency to chase squirrels adds up to a juicy diagnosis. And if Mitzi were human she'd own shares in GlaxoSmithKline, for her drug schedule is ornate, not to mention her diet. As Rosa departs for the gym in spring-loaded runners she hands Alanna Mitzi's schedule for the day.

7 AM: Pawlates DVD plus run on beach (pink Bernouli jacket)

8 AM: Ritalin, Paxil, ginseng, powdered kale, pulverized calf liver

9 AM: Buttermilk bath, Thai massage

1 AM: On-set readiness class with life coach Jake (jaunty T-shirt!)

1 PM: Vitamin injection, grapefruit juice, bleeding bison protein shake

2 PM: Private yoga tutorial (Downward Dog Enterprises)

3 PM: Cognitive challenge games, sign language practice

4 PM: Nap time, hypnobedience CD (Good dog!)

6 PM: Mommy gets home! Dinner and dog treats on the deck

"Whew! Quite the agenda," whistles Char, brewing herself up a skim-milk latte. The nanny suite, directly below the

penthouse, came equipped with Blue Ray, high-speed broad-
band, a sculpted marble Jacuzzi, but what really excites Char
is the kitchen where brand-new juicers, espresso makers and
microwaves are lined up. "Take your pick," said Dawn last
night, off-handedly. "Whatever you don't want we'll pass on
to charity." That also went for the stack of DVDs, unworn
yoga kit and designer footwear piled up on the sleek white
leather couch. After gorging themselves on complimentary
sushi, the sisters spent an intoxicating few hours trying on
lycra bra tops and snakeskin wedge heels while listening to
top-ten disco hits of the seventies and eighties. This morning
Char decided to whip up bennies, try out some of the unused
all-clad copper-core cooking pans she's unearthed from the
spotless ground floor cupboards. After that she plans to go
shopping. Maybe look for a laptop she can work from home
on. Plus it's time to get going on some MBA applications. All
this announced to Alanna in breathless excitement "because
you, my dear, are so much better with animals."

Ugh, yikes, bad hair day.

"What?"

I said, I look like shit.

"Is that Char?" Alanna searches the penthouse for her sister, ends up back in the dog's room, where she started. Dawn
and Rosa have long since left and she is already running an
hour behind schedule. Rain pelts cynically against the windows and meanwhile Mitzi lounges listlessly in her day bed,
gazing at her reflection in some chrome chair legs. Not an
auspicious start to her new engagement, and now this, an
aural hallucination. For the gruff, whiny voice, like that of a
chain-smoking toddler, is clearly not coming from anyone
else.

"I'm not psychic, you know. That was just an experiment."

Yeah, well, whatever.

Alanna decides to move on to Mitzi's breakfast. Her cell phone already reads 8:18 and she's yet to figure out the complex blister packs. Maybe she should just take the drugs herself. And the kale too, why not, she's never actually eaten it and maybe it would do her body some good. But she draws the line at calf liver: for both of them.

"We're going for Pedigree Chum, my friend. It's cheaper and easier. I bought some on my way here – I'm sure you'll like it. Way tastier and junkier than mashed up calf liver and that way I don't have to get my fingernails bloody." She opens the can of all-beef chunks and empties it into Mitzi's monogrammed dog bowl, praying her employers will not check their recycling and also that the voice does not recur. She did not mean to begin breaking rules this early, but these, she tells herself, are exceptional circumstances. The calf liver she will deal with later.

But Mitzi pushes the bowl away, retches pathetically.

I want to kill myself.

"What?" Alanna puts the liver back down on the counter.

You heard me.

"Jesus, it *is* you, isn't it!"

I thought you hated people. Don't you want to help?

"Listen, Mitz, you're a dog, not a person. And anyway, I'm no Doctor Kevorkian. I came here to work, to keep you alive."

Great. Another trainer, the last thing I need.

"Don't you *want* to be in show biz?"

Mitzi turns her head away and pukes. Cleaning it up, Alanna feels cold in the pit of her stomach. She remembers her mother, a drooling mess, rocking back and forth on the cockeyed sofa. Far from the concert pianist her parents raised her to be, Jay was a mental patient, and not a good one; she flubbed up her meds, resulting in mood swings so sharp she could shift outlook completely between sentence fragments. After Doug hit his fateful moose she was deemed incompetent of person, and after the girls escaped into care was swallowed whole by some psychiatric establishment, the kind that only spits you out in a box.

One day Jay will do herself in. It's all just a matter of time and smuggled contraband. That much is clear, although the sisters do not admit to it. Contorted by guilt, Alanna strokes Mitzi's curls, pulls their funky spirals into weird shapes. The dog is warm, her breath reassuring and even. And now that the truth is out, Alanna senses a degree of canine elation. Perhaps she is Mitzi's first ever confidante, a sad fact, given how extensive her pampering. When Mitzi next speaks it is in a growl, a sign, thinks Alanna, that the animal feels more herself. Buoyed by this, Alanna fetches a leash, declares it's time to go walkies; and while she's at it she cancels Mitzi's appointments, informing Jake the life coach that Mitzi is unwell. Jake snaps back, "Don't you know I have a 24-hour cancellation policy?" but seems willing to let it go when Alanna promises payment, on condition he issue a tax receipt as per usual. By noon she and Mitz are on Second Beach, romping in the waves and digging ditches. It's drizzling still, but nothing a long-term Vancouverite can't handle, and Alanna lets Mitzi play outdoors naked, something the dog has not done for quite some time.

"Oh my God, where's her coat?" It's Char, dressed in a brand new outfit.

"I donated it to charity; the boots, also."

"Well, well, well, aren't we the fast mover."

Char's tone sets Alanna on edge. "Speak for yourself, Miss Holt Renfrew." Ankle-length coat, patent boots, suede purse: it's clear Char has dropped a couple of thousand since exiting the apartment with her new travel mug, money the twins do not yet have in hand. Char always did like to rack up debt, even as a kid, "investing" in fashionable clothes by borrowing off boyfriends, paying them back with her body, or not at all. When she and Alanna moved in together, Alanna made her sign a contract not to get into debt under any circumstances. Char said that was cool, she was not into conflict, but now she is clearly making up for lost time.

"Well, I'm going back. Have to make a few important phone calls. Then it's my shift, isn't it? I'm not going to waste this fabulous chance by cheating our employers out of what they paid for."

"Why don't you just take the whole day off?"

"Fine." Char swivels, lurches, marches up to the steps to dry land again.

Please don't leave me alone with her, begs Mitzi.

"Don't worry, I won't."

The next few days, Char disappears into what she calls her new office, the apartment's second bedroom, emerges every now and then, grinning. It seems she has used this change of pace to kick-start her career as a corporate companion.

"No more kissy-kissy," she declares. "This is all hands-off, strictly symbolic. They pay me to look fabulous, impress their colleagues, and that's that." Meanwhile her wardrobe expands exponentially. Shopping trips and "networking" sessions take up all of Char's afternoons and increasingly Alanna is left alone with Mitzi. Together they gorge on fish and chips, visit bowling alleys and obscure dog parks, mingle closely with the canine unwashed to such an extent that Alanna has to bathe her, use up tube after tube of Buttermilk Bonewash to make sure Mitzi smells right to her loving parents, who stay at work longer and longer every evening, eventually staying out all night. Alanna doesn't mind: her charge's musky, mud-and-leather aroma fills her with glee. Plus Mitzi is a great listener. Alanna finds herself indulging in rambling anecdotes, detailed descriptions of her mother's cooking (tuna casserole, corn dogs, ketchup sandwiches) and the kinds of songs she used to sing when happy enough to get through all the verses. Meanwhile Mitzi stops vomiting, communicates in regular barks and yaps. Yet it seems to Alanna they still share spirit worlds, hazy places full of complex smells and textures increasingly the topic of her daydreams, as if instead of Mitzi becoming a person, she was turning happily into a great cockapoo, exchanging the city for some ancestral savannah across which packs of animals traveled in concert, ignorant of aesthetics and net worth.

Then, on the fifth day, Rosa comes home.

"Where's Dawn? What do you mean, she's at work? For 72 hours?"

"That's what she told me."

Rosa, fresh from L.A., is a mess of right angles, her knees bent as if about to butt-kick the universe. "That's bullshit, sweetheart."

Seven phone calls later, the truth emerges. Dawn is having an affair with her personal assistant, a blond, named Spike, of indeterminate gender. In short order, Rosa discovers the Chum tins, interrogates Jake and sniffs out buried dog clothes, is appalled that Mitzi has missed her one big audition, a screen test for the part of a corpse in a Hollywood romantic comedy; Jonathan Demme supposedly directing. It was Rosa's big break.

"But Mitzi and I were having fun."

"*This dog is gifted.*" Rosa hisses. As Mitzi is stuffed into clown hat and ruff and strapped down ruthlessly in her new stroller, Alanna feels nauseous.

"That's cruel. That's …" she almost says *child abuse*, heads to the bathroom to vomit up Kool-Aid, Kraft dinner, Mitzi's tortured child-voice bouncing off the antique wash stand: *I can't fucking stand this, Alanna. Kill me.*

"No way, Mitzi, no way. Why don't you kill Rosa?"

The next day Alanna and Char are out on the street. Char has had to give back most of her clothing, which she'd somehow managed to charge to Rosa's credit card. Her neck is scarred with love bites and her buttocks with whip marks, evidence of companionship gone bestial. But still she refuses to quit.

"I'm going hooking."

"You are not."

"Yes sirree, back to old Rick. I know he'll give my job back if I beg for it. But not for long: I swear, I am headed for business school, just as soon as I pay off my debts, and then, dear Al, you'll be amazed."

"Okay, fine. But Char, keep in touch."

"I will."

Char hugs Alanna, lightly, like you would an invalid, and heads out into the grungy puddles of Granville Street, leaving Alanna alone again on the sidewalk, listening to the emptiness inside her head.

Where I Live Now

I

In the first photograph it's a cold Sunday afternoon in late February, 1977. The dull, flat landscape of the back garden is enlivened by lurid outbreaks of crocus in Parma violet mauve and custard yellow, the odd emerald encrustation of moss. My father crouches in the cabbage patch, holds his right hand out to an English robin that cocks its head to one side. Above them swings a tube of raw peanuts, its plastic mesh pecked to shreds by hungry sparrows. The bird table it hangs off hosts a starling slick with rain while beside the beech hedge, unmoving yet watchful, I curl my toes up and down inside my wellies and refuse to admit to myself the awful truth.

II

Standing up to my full height of six feet two inches I almost bang my head on the luggage locker before retrieving my backpack and shuffling down the aisle towards rickety steps then solid ground. The air is hot and wet like that in a sauna and it's hard to believe this is England, 1998. The bus doors close with a wheeze and I sit down hard, wonder what Dad ate for his last meal. I remember his voice, barely audible over the long-distance phone line, begging me for Mackeson's stout, despite the fact that I am in Canada where beer is drunk light and cold, that photo of him holding a mince pie up to some other old codger's mouth, his sweater slipping off his skeletal shoulders, loose as a butterfly's cocoon. The returning prodigal, muscled and fit from years schlepping up and down raw mountains, photographing insects, collecting samples of moths, beetles and flies, I could not say if he was happy then.

Where I live now the snow is pure and bright and the blue amber of glaciers freezes time into delicate, folded crags. I set my watch by the long dash, eat kale regularly. When not outdoors, I spend my days in air-conditioned rooms, crouched over microscopes, adjusting the legs of ants with steel tweezers while counting up lesions, my face pressed into the eyepiece, away from light. After work I run around the seawall, watch British sitcoms on TV, occasionally make love with a fellow scientist whose size eleven runners stink up my hallway but whose red sauce is excellent. Neither of us marches: Brian because of his mother, me – well, me, I'm not a joiner. Nor am I a patriot: I do not miss Marmite, never feel nostalgic, speak with a mid-Atlantic accent and hold only one passport. The child in the garden seems far away, a character in a Mike Leigh movie, his repressed father a cliché in Brylcreem and slacks.

"Watch your bag, mate!" A man shields his toddler from my sharp-edged briefcase as the airport bus pulls into the gate and its doors slide open, admit haze and glare. I wince at his flattened cadences, their downward slide provoking a fit of breathlessness as if a bird is trapped in my chest, in my house.

When I arrive the curtains are closed. No one has lived here for six weeks, since Dad collapsed in the kitchen, his boil-in-the-bag cod in cheese sauce reduced to a mess of burnt plastic by the time his neighbour Mrs. Dutton noticed the awful smell. I sense her now, a birdlike presence behind her living room curtain, alert to the rattle of the spare key in the lock, the swish of Dad's front door opening across carpet, my graceless skid across the envelopes accumulated behind the letterbox, their bulk as unexpected as snow in June. *Dear Mr. Royal, You have won an all expenses paid trip for two to Dublin.* A tightly furled umbrella with a wooden handle, a glass ashtray, two left worn-out old men's slippers, tucked between them a handwritten cardboard notice: NO MILK TODAY.

After struggling with the locks on the double glazing I open windows, stuff rancid sheets and towels into the doll-sized washer and do my best to ignore the floral note-card propped open on the kitchen table: *Hello Dear. Give me a tinkle if you need anything. Love Sue.* The lady vicar insisted Dad was deeply missed. Yet my guess is, other than the old folks he spent Tuesday afternoons with at the Lodge, he would go for weeks without seeing anyone. One kitchen cupboard is filled with small tins of soup, their labels all turned outward at the same angle. My latest card, two timber wolves in deep snow, recycled paper, sits alone beside a postcard from Bournemouth on the mantelpiece. *Dear Dad*, I remember writing. *Whistler is crowded.* The postcard, from a now-dead cousin, is five years old.

I have only six days to clear out the house and prepare it for sale. I could have taken longer, but my research is at a crucial stage and the next month or so could be critical. Overwhelmed suddenly, I sit down at the kitchen table and lay my head against its cool veneer. The kettle clicks off. I remember a TV documentary from years ago that ran together clips of British actors, each one asking, Shall I make a cup of tea? as the crises grew more and more extreme. I stand up, open a box of PG Tips and drop two bags into the teapot. Although scalding hot, the tea tastes of ash. I pour it down the drain.

III

It's the photos I want. I could pretend otherwise, will, when Mrs. Dutton inevitably pops round, or the reverend Sue, armed with blurry leaflets, active listening. It's not that they don't mean well. It's just that the full scope of this is invisible to the naked eye, my father's corpse a Russian doll that conceals within it certain others. *If only they knew* – this the phrase I catch myself thinking, as if I were eleven, not thirty-two, yet the truth is even I don't know, for my father was a stranger to me, even at his most intimate, and now that he is gone all I can do is attempt to reconstruct the possibilities, an anthropologist examining old bones.

The second day, after an early morning run along narrow sidewalks, I go through Dad's photo albums in systematic fashion. A picture of Mum on holiday in the Lakes catches me up short, as does one of the three of us in silly party hats, and at lunchtime I find myself making a trip to the Co-op for a pack of Dunhill then retching into the toilet, although the smell on Dad's clothes becomes less noxious afterwards, as if two puffs have rendered me immune. Emboldened, I ransack his garden shed then the closet in the spare bedroom, which is where I find the boxes of slides. Bingo.

The house backs onto a school field, and while I sit on the duvet, holding each white frame up to the light, children's voices drift in through the window, their uniformed bodies erratic variables acting upon a constant of burnt, brown grass.

IV

"Come with me to work," says Dad one Wednesday morning, about a month after my mother's death. I hate Wednesdays: double French plus double PE equals quadruple humiliation and since I've been back at school everyone avoids me except for Susan Baines who is obsessed with grief, probably because she has never, ever lost anything. Even her woolly hats are attached with string. So although the smell of gas makes me sick and the scratching of mice against plastic gives me the creeps I agree to accompany Dad to the college that morning, to sit in his stinky office between labs sketching rats on computer paper while he teaches sexual reproduction to Sixth Form dropouts. It seems to make him happy and I know the drill: pretend I have a cold if anyone asks, ignore the creepy skeleton, laugh at Dad's jokes.

"Are you all right?" He asks in the car.

"Of course I am," I lie. The drafty office brings me out in goose pimples. It's only when his voice has faded into theatrical sing-song, thrilling words like "gamete" and "ovum" blurring into humdrum gobbledegook that I slip down off the high stool he has sat me on and prowl around the room, in search of love.

Three years ago, Dad had an affair with a blonde-haired student named Heidi. I know this because I found a picture of her pinned up inside the door of the garden shed. I knew Heidi a little bit. She had been over to our house once the previous summer, supposedly for a last-minute tutorial. Placing the rake to one side, I hunched down under the makeshift window for a moment, ignoring the fact that the air stank of creosote, and remembered how Heidi's warm white hair smelt of black cherry yogurt before sliding her picture coolly inside my vest. Later I hid it face-down inside the red velvet jewellery box Grandma once gave me, intending to reflect on it later, Heidi's presence in the shed being too much, at that point, to take in. But when I next opened my box the photo had vanished. I never did find out where it went.

I rifle halfheartedly through the papers on Dad's desk, whisper out loud the word "Memorandum," catch my foot on the corner of one of the battered green filing cabinets and a large, scruffy envelope falls out. I kneel down and pick it up, expecting to find coded letters, pictures of Heidi or perhaps just notes on sexual reproduction but the clatter of plastic frames is a surprise – why would Dad hide pictures of plants? For close-ups of weeds and wild flowers are the only shots he ever converts into slides. There must be something mysterious about these. Rare species? I lift one up into a shaft of light spiraling towards me between dying cacti, angle the blotchy, darkened membrane carefully until its secret finally comes into view.

V

In the second photograph, a boy of about six bends over the side of a bathtub, his tiny buttocks naturally parted. Harmless enough, you might think. But what happens next? The boy is taken into a neighbouring room. The boy's father grabs his little leg and yanks it, exposing the child's penis. Then he rubs, chafing with callused fingers until it stiffens.

Shadowy, cavernous, suspended intact from the surface of his skull, the walls of the cage the boy retreats into are reinforced so well no thought can penetrate, no information from tongue, skin. All that exists there is light, dark, sound and knowledge. From this refuge the boy watches carefully as his father turns the camera on.

"Get up." Fear shimmers, a greasy patch. The boy gets into position, hands and knees, head facing forward. The next sequence is confusing, a blur of bodies. There's a close-up of brown blood, smeared on the father's penis and the carpet. Then the father places his hands around the boy's neck, whispers, "Don't tell," and weeps long and hard into his fist.

Then lens caps are replaced, films removed and placed into soft cloth bags before slowly, as slowly as snow falls, the boy descends to reunite with himself. He does not know what will happen next or if the smell of carpet will continue to haunt him, only that his father won't touch him now the distance between them is astral, infinite, the man closed up, his dark matter hidden, a reality science can't grapple with, at least not yet.

VI

"Chips or mashed potato?"

"Chips, please." The woman behind the counter shovels some onto my plate and I smile at her.

"Nice lad, i'n't he?" she says, winking at Dad. At this time of night the college cafeteria is echoey, most of the students having already left. We stayed on to clean out the cages of the salamanders, plus Dad hates home. He says the living room wallpaper's full of faces, Mum's and his from happier days. After a think I decided not to argue. At least the food is edible out here.

"Give the lad some cake."

The woman grins, picks out the fattest wedge of Black Forest Gateau, slides it expertly onto a styrofoam platter. It looks great, but the cream is actually off and after Dad has finally gone to bed I vomit it all back up in semi-darkness then switch the light on to count at least six black cherries afloat in our filthy toilet bowl, their purple-reddish clusters like gouts of blood.

My father is kind. My father is nice. My father works hard and lets me sleep in on the weekends, weeds flower beds, rakes leaves and converses with neighbours about the inclement weather while I jack off to pictures of men being whipped, photographs of photographs I copy from the History section of the library, imagine myself sliced into quarters, halves. For boys like me the world is a good place, safe and calm except for the escalating arms race, acne and Thatcherism. Memory comes back to us much later, in the form of a spotlight focused on our third eyes as we fuck other would-be scientists, high on acid or stoned on Moroccan black, a light that reveals our pathetic young genitals, tender as jellyfish, grasped in the hands of the man whose surname we carry. We refuse to utter it, instead when the light blinks off move as far away as possible, to America first then finally Canada, a dog-eared folder full of animal sketches and a jam jar filled with old cat ashes the only souvenirs we choose to take.

VII

"So what made you an entomologist?" Brian rattles his Rolex, pets his brush cut. We are in the Pink Pearl one rainy morning, plates of dim sum laid out neatly between us. It's our first real date. Terrified, I attack my chopsticks with gusto, probe a steaming dumpling, extract its meat.

"Mm-mm, delicious." I swallow slippery fat, unclench my buttocks. There's no use getting tense: they always sense it. I take a deep breath. "As far as I recall, it was a photograph."

"What of?"

"I don't remember exactly. Some fancy beetle. My Dad taught college-level Biology. I was ransacking his office. The photo was in a file that fell down on top of me. I could draw that, I thought, could draw it better, all I would need to do is sketch it from life."

"So you did."

"Yes, though not till I came here."

"So it wasn't native?"

"No, no, you could say that."

VIII

Our fairytale begins at a conference in Florida, where I present on jewel beetles. After I've delivered my verdict – pink-headeds will soon be extinct, barring aberrant pockets in the sub-alpine – I feel sick to my stomach. Undergraduates bring out my inner misanthrope, the part of me that chants, Bring it on! And the crowd at the campus café that day seems particularly puerile. Indulging in a chocolate-chip cookie while contemplating flights back to Toronto, I'm trying to avoid some tanned young thing juggling muffins between the cash registers when a man I recognize as the presenter of Biology as Destiny: Arachnid Predation Under Duress taps me on the shoulder.

"Hey, Grub Man, fancy a trip into town?"

"Sure, why not." I offered my free hand.

"Brian Goldenberg, a.k.a. Spiderman."

"Pleased to meet you." About my height but at least twenty pounds heavier, he exudes a calm that entrances me from the start.

And so it comes to pass that my white knight and I head into Tampa, specifically the Museum of Art where an awful exhibition of medical photographs is on display. Later, after ogling sweet specimens in Skateboard Park we make our way to Ybor City, to an upscale leather bar Brian insists is a cocktail lounge before I point out the studded banquettes.

"Not my scene."

"Nor mine."

"Ah, well."

We return to home base. Examining Brian under the fluorescent lights of the student residence lobby, it occurs to me he is utterly, frighteningly beautiful.

"Listen," he says. "I've had a great time."

"So have I. Want to keep in touch?"

"Sure."

"Here's my card." As I tuck it into his breast pocket he kisses me deeply.

It turns out we are separated by a border: one that will matter later; perhaps too much.

IX

"So, what's it like in Canada?"

"Full of igloos," I reply.

Marge grins, a few Digestive crumbs still stuck around her wizened mouth. She's aged well, the Donny Osmond hats replaced by furtive blonde streaks, chunky jewelry, bright white T-shirts and Capri's. She must be over seventy but the cracks aren't showing yet, except when she stares at me with shock-wide eyes.

"She was a card, your mum. Always good for a laugh." I think Marge is about to cry when instead she sneezes, wipes foundation off along with snot and stares back, red-nosed. "Did you hear about the college?"

"You mean the merger?" My heart races unexpectedly. I think about all the grey underpants I just binned, the black socks, the copies of *Reader's Digest*.

"No, no, love, that was years ago!" Marge leans close, over the pile of mail I've just redirected. An ant surfaces through the crust of the sugar bowl. "No, no, love, I mean the porn-*og*raphy scandal." The way she pronounces the word amuses, at least for a second. It can't be *him* she's talking about. *Recipient Deceased.*

"It was all over the papers. Some fellow who'd been working there for years. Turned out he was one of them peda-gogues. And there was money in it. A computer ring, you know." Cold tea curdling in her cup, Marge watches my face for a reaction. I do not give one.

"Your father – was he, you know … I mean, did he ever …" She puts her hands up. "Not that I'm insinuating! It's just that …" Marge reaches out across the wipe-clean tablecloth, takes my trembling hand in hers, presses her three gold rings, engagement, wedding and eternity against my knuckles – "I saw this photograph."

"What photograph?"

"A snap of a boy in a funny pose, you know …" She puts her hand on her hip, purses her lips and lolls provocatively. "This was years ago. It was stuffed into a book."

"And was the boy me?" I consider pulling out my album, holding up the worst slides to the light, perhaps even closing the curtains, running a little kiddie porn on the walls. This is my chance, I think, for some vindication. But then the dark side of me steps in.

"Get out," I say, pulling my hand away. "Please, please, Margery, just get the hell out."

"Listen, dear, I know you're upset!" Marge stands with a creak, extricates herself from behind the table. "I just want you to know I don't bear a grudge. The funeral and all that, even his body – I was happy to do it. He was her man. You are her son. No one can say I'm not loyal." She dabs her eyes again, readjusts her necklace. "Of course I was shocked. I mean, when I thought … when I realized." She grabs my arm, sinks her frosted nails into my suntan. "I did think of saying something. But your mother … she would have been devastated! I couldn't tell her, could I? I mean we never talked about it, not in those days. What would she have done?"

"She could have left him."

Just then the doorbell rings. I look up, through the open door into the living room, see a heavyset woman nursing a pile of leaflets bob nervously up and down outside the locked front door.

"It's the Reverend," whispers Marge. Neither of us moves. The doorbell rings again then a couple of leaflets land softly on the empty doormat. The woman crosses back in front of the window, disappears down the garden path.

Marge releases my arm. There are indentations. "Please leave," I repeat.

"All right love, keep your hair on." She sneaks a peek at herself in the kitchen window before backing awkwardly out through my father's living room, scooping up her handbag from off the hall floor then stepping carefully over the Reverend's leaflets as if afraid to dirty herself on them.

X

Nine months after Tampa, Bri is visiting. We're out on my tiny patio, sipping an Australian Shiraz. Brian seems nervous, distracted. Turns out he has a job offer from a rival establishment, the über-groovy uni up on the hill.

"I've got my work permit and everything."

I say nothing. Meanwhile he twinkles, expectant.

"What's the matter? I thought you wanted us to move in!"

Steady now, says Mum, pressing up behind me. Her pale fingers graze mine. I shiver, disoriented, turn away and pretend to examine my herb pots. She asked me once about a bloodstain in my underpants. I stared back, pretended I had no idea. Another time three rolls of film fell out of the refrigerator and instead of pleading for help I scooped them up quickly, terrified she'd hold them to the light.

Brian jerks his foot forward, spills his Shiraz. "God damn it! Why are you so changeable? Is there something you're not saying?"

"Yes." No word seems more futile.

"Oh I see, so you're a closet pedophile and the apartment is stuffed full of crack."

"There is an awful lot you don't know." *Watch out,* says Dad. *I'll kill you if you tell.* My heart speeds up; there's a sudden rise in temperature like an avalanche warning.

I'm about to leave when something soft brushes against my ankle: a perfect tortoiseshell, yellow eyes staring out if its wings. Just as suddenly they fold, turning the creature back into darkness.

"Listen, love, want me to mop this up?"

"Sure." As Brian bends to blot the wine with his napkin, I notice his perfect fingernails, pure white and crescent shaped. What was his father like? Did he touch him? What kind of man would raise someone so clean?

XI

I'm an anxious child. I live in fear of the unknown – other children, death, the skip behind the off-licence, what will happen to my cat when I leave home at eighteen. At the age of eleven, six months before my mother dies I steal half her sleeping pills, stash them in a film canister and lodge it between the slats of my bed, plan to take them all in one go just before the world ends, but when it finally does they've fallen out and been crushed, presumably by the weight of my dreams, which are mostly of Armageddon anyway.

At fourteen my shoulders slump, my hair is greasy, a head-banger's. If there's one thing I can't stand it's the feeling of someone looking at me. I'm clever enough not to let people know my proclivities but that doesn't mean I feel pride. I hate my mouth because it's so girly, my hands because they crack, bleed and can't keep still. On my very first date I wear fingerless gloves, choose the darkest table in the King's Head to lecture fat Goth Keith Harris on nuclear fission. We prick CND symbols into our knuckles with a KISS pin then practice duck and cover, huddling beneath tables until the landlord finally chucks us out.

"So what do *you* want to be?" Keith asks on the way home, bitter, ironic. A cheap gilt crucifix hangs out over his jacket. Spring stars glisten. His lipstick is black and intact.

"Male porn star or mad scientist, I'm not sure which." I walk beside him now, but at a distance, afraid he might ask to be touched.

"Oi, slow down!" Keith lights a fag and we sit together on the low wall outside the butcher's, smoke it together in turns like a joint.

"How about you?"

"Drag queen," he whispers. I exhale slowly.

"That full moon would probably smash, should it fall to earth."

XII

Dear Brian,

I never did tell so here it goes. The lad's name was Toby Steinberg. He was gorgeous, of course, big grin, massive pecs ... I thought he was eighteen, nineteen but it turned out he was quite a bit older, had had a kid with his high school sweetheart. One day he asked could he bring his son to class. Of course I agreed. The kid was about seven or eight, white-blond hair. The class went fine, all the girls doting on Junior. I can't remember exactly what we were studying, possibly exoskeletons. Anyway, after we were done I was wiping off the chalkboard when the kid comes back all by himself. Turned out he'd left his Pokémon under a chair or something. So he looks me in the eyes, says please, and all at once I want to rescue him. Not Toby Steinberg, his son. Have you seen Pikachu? Yes, I have. He's still squeaking away under that chair. The boy shambles over to retrieve his toy. I hyperventilate. Who is in more trouble, him or me? A few minutes later we are back outside and Toby Steinberg is anxiously thanking me. I nod my head. I don't know what to do so I go back into the classroom, into the store cupboard, and for some reason think of my Dad, which turns me on so bad I slam the door and jack off right then and there, but it isn't enjoyable, in fact it's awful, and all I can think to myself is what the hell is happening? What the fucking hell is going on?

XIII

After Marge leaves I close the curtains, slap Perry Como on the turntable, weep hard and long into the living room floor, then collapse in a heap. The phone rings several times but I don't answer. Instead I take my clothes off, put them on again, call Brian and listen to his voice.

"Thanks for calling. Spiderman isn't home now. If you'd like to leave a message, do so after the beep." He said I could call if I needed to. He's visiting his mother. She also lives in Seattle (we didn't move in). Before Dad died, things were going great between us. The only problem I had was sleeplessness.

Dear Beloved Students,

Now that we have sacrificed our final dung beetles, let us step back and review the field as a whole. In particular let us consider biological science, how the urge to know transforms into the need to manipulate, place the self that caresses beside the self that assaults and coolly investigate; only then might a theory to encompass them be devised.

After writing this I slug back some vodka, retrieve the offending slides from the corner whatnot, stuff all my unmailed letters into an envelope, scrawl Brian's name and address on it, shove my feet into flip-flops and head outside.

After depositing the envelope in a postbox, I cut through the lane behind the church and scurry across the main road towards the cemetery. Thank God nobody stops to say hello. There are plenty of shoppers out, some smeared with ice cream, but the heat's sufficient to dull their outrage, their nerve.

Dear Brian,

I thought coming here would help me get clear on the darkness, the locked room where the worst of me still lives. Instead it has grown increasingly hard to stay present.

Dressed only in boxers, I dash through the cemetery's wrought iron gate. Mum's small gravestone is on the left, beneath an elm I recognize then immediately hesitate: it's no lush green icon. The sun has shriveled its long grass down to sandpaper, its leaves into arthritic, brittle hands. Also, the new grave beside it, Dad's, has no headstone. Its earth is oddly dented, completely dried out. I was expecting something fresher, rawer, a wound made in reality, letting nightmares through.

Boy, eight, eyes closed, naked on carpet. The back bedroom, the one kept locked during the day, was supposedly Dad's office but he never used it. I broke in twice and was surprised to find it full of empty suitcases, no cameras anywhere in sight.

Man, forty-three, eyes open, callused hands encircling boy's neck. When I first discovered pink-headed beetles, I wanted to defend them against all destroyers: pesticides, herbicides, bikers, entomologists, the sun. Then Dad died and I found I was one of them anyway, shifting their cells around as if I were God.

First I get out the picture I've chosen to put on Mum's grave: the snap of us in silly hats. I bet she'd like that. Then I lie down in the dry earth under the elm trees, the photo of Dad and the robin pressed to my chest. It's quiet here, mercifully free of eyes. No doubt someone will track me down eventually, cart me away and lock me up, as they should.

The Stockholm Syndrome

ONE TUESDAY, Susan locked the dog in the basement. She thought it was time she did something for herself. She went down twice a day with his leash or some dog treats, only to disappear and not come back. In this way and others she teased him horribly and then she left him down there for a week. The dog, Mortimer, a lab-collie mix, was alternately terrified, almost hysterical, and catatonic. She would hear him howling, leaping at the stairwell then suddenly all would go quiet. She would fear he was dead. She would pace about upstairs, put on loud music, anything to get him to react. But as soon as he started up again, she would curse him. Stupid dog! Stupid fucking Mortimer! Why had her parents left her here alone with him? How long, exactly, until he starved?

Susan loved dogs. She loved every one of God's creatures. She was a cheerleader as well as a Christian plus on the Honour Roll at school. Yet after Tuesday she also knew she was evil. Or else why would she be mean, why would she be doing this. Perhaps this meant she no longer had to wear braces, could rip them out of her mouth and simply roar. There were girls at school who snorted cocaine, others who already had babies, and all because of low self-esteem. Personally, Susan hated her kneecaps, which weren't really kneecaps at all but folds of flesh that hung down and touched each other and

117

made her walk funny. She also hated her hair, the colour of weak tea and so oily it often appeared sodden, flakes of dandruff kebabbed along its shafts.

She did not hate her boyfriend, Michael. She craved him. But she knew he did not respect her the way he should. For example, he criticized her clothing and whenever she reached for a pretzel grabbed her hand. That's enough. You've had too many already. They had sex standing up in his parents' kitchen while his parents were out in their car making love also. All four felt closer to God that way. But despite the fact that his parents were both athletes, Michael fucked with little finesse. Yet after they had finished, he and Susan prayed together and this she found intensely moving. The linoleum was sticky and cold. Michael's pink acne ran right down his neck and across his back. As they knelt together, Susan had to restrain herself from picking at it, from pressing each little volcano between her fingers, for fear something horrible might erupt.

On the fourth day of his captivity, Mortimer escaped. He barreled up the stairs, knocking her over, made straight for the plastic bin of dog food and gorged himself until he threw up. Whenever she came near he whined, as if he could see the devil on her shoulder, grinning and twirling its blood-red, horned batons. While Mortimer leapt about begging for exercise Susan attempted to achieve enlightenment. She sat on the wobbly IKEA chair rocking backward and forward, backward and forward, repeating the word "home" until it said womb. And when her parents got home from Hawaii they glowed with affection, not for her but for themselves, although they were full up enough for some to spill over. Their suitcases on wheels were covered in stickers. They stumbled around as if suffering from hangovers. They had brought her a lei.

Six months later, Susan left home. She had yet to complete high school. She knew she would live to regret this but felt something had gone missing, something non-negotiable: her body, herself. She got rid of her faith, her cheerleader costume and Michael. She dyed her hair turquoise, moved to a hostel, gave her name as Jinx and her hometown as Oshawa, decided she would like to move to L.A. One day she made it as far as the Greyhound depot where she met a man called Anton, with a weird accent. Anton-with-a-weird-accent said he was a refugee. He was skinny and tall and his hair stood out, a wild red burning bush. His voice seemed to emanate from it. She believed that voice, became lulled by it, and within a couple of hours had moved into the condemned walkup where he lived.

At first he told her there were gangsters after him. That was why she had to do as he said. She was a middle class girl from the suburbs who did not understand how to behave and anything she did or said could be suspect. Anton stole food and clothing and lived on rice wine, anything fermented he could get his hands on yet claimed he was a poet. He wrote in tiny, unlined spiral-bound notebooks using a leaky Hello Kitty ballpoint, line after line of poetry she could not read. One day she stole a book of her own and began writing lists in it, countries she would like to run cafes in, brands of salad dressing she missed and yearned for, but Anton found it and ripped it up, said he was the writer, she should not forget that. Shortly after, he began locking her in, taking the key to the door and disappearing for hours. When he came home he would ask what she had been up to. Had she turned on the lights? Had she peed? Had she masturbated? Meanwhile his body, its sinew-wrapped bones became the only diagram she could relate to. She lived for his touch, his hollowed-out eyes, the slap and suck of their

119

Something About the Animal

flesh cleaving together. So what if he bruised her? He always apologized. She did not know any word for this but bliss.

No, it didn't need repeating, although he said it often, *I love you, I love you*, as if he himself could barely believe it, the feelings he had for this (according to the mirror) sulky adolescent whose dye job was growing out and whose hip bones were showing, poking their noses out and into his business. Yet one day, two months later, Susan moved out. Anton, fatally, had left the door unlocked. Observing this, Susan rinsed her mouth out with cold, rancid coffee, laced up her Docs and casually sauntered forward. As she paused in the doorway Anton leapt up from the couch. Where the fuck you going? Susan could not think of a destination. He grabbed her collar. Go, said Anton, releasing his grip. She fell backwards. Another inch and she would have slid down the stairs. Go, bitch. She knew he must be hurting. God knew what terrible crimes he had witnessed or even been party to back in his homeland. She, on the other hand, was a blank slate. What had she ever done except leave home? He loved her, he said. He did not want to hurt her. No one was going to accuse him of that. Back where he came from pride was important. And he knew one day she would marry and have children and that her future husband would not be him. He just wanted to help her. Was she safe? She looked at the marks on her hands and around her ankles where Anton had them with rope and still wasn't sure.

Go, he said. It was easy to leave. Ridiculously easy, all things considered. She did not have luggage. She just had her clothes. Anton had said that was all *he* had. She pictured him, an orange cloud, receding slowly up towards the snowline before descending down into neutral territory. His notebook, his coat. As she herself limped down, down, Anton stayed put, staring into the chasm of the stairwell.

120

When she arrived home after walking all night her mother slammed the door in her face then opened it again quickly. Come inside, she hissed, before anyone sees you. Just then a neighbour drove past in a silver minivan, almost swerved right off the road.

All that day, her parents circled her warily, as if she were a werewolf, about to grow fur. *We've been worried sick. We've been praying hard. The whole congregation has.* Her mother hugged her. *Wow, you smell awful. What have you been eating? We kept your room. It feels like years. You could go back to school in September. Look at your hair. Have you had unsafe sex? I knew Jesus was listening to me, I knew it.* Whenever Susan went outside she experienced reverse celebrity, like a sex offender or a suspected terrorist. She became convinced she could hear other people's thoughts. *Oh my God, look at that child! Is she on crystal meth? How ungrateful!* In the mall people backed away as if they could smell Anton on her fingers.

That summer was hot. She agreed to see the counselor her parents found and ended up on various legal drugs, psychoactive substances she'd taken on the street but now was having paid for by her parents. The shrink was young and handsome. He liked to touch her shoulder when she cried.

A few weeks later, Mortimer was run over by a car. Her parents buried him in the back yard. One night she tried to dig him up, stood there in the warm air in her nightshirt stamping on a wooden shovel but to no avail. The ground had gone hard. Mortimer might as well not have existed. The next day Michael her ex came over to visit. He informed her she was paranoid schizophrenic, always had been and probably always would be. He was standing on top of Mortimer's grave in his shirtsleeves, off to med school in the fall and seeing another cheerleader named Sara. Michael said there were some good drugs. Susan said she was already on them. He wished her a normal life, even shaking her hand before walking back to his brand new Volvo, a graduation present from his parents who were heading out on mission in their Winnebago. Michael looked very young behind the wheel. Susan wondered if Sara popped his acne. Later, drunk on vodka, she decided to kill him. Meanwhile she would act really nice.

Susan got a job in a café making sandwiches. What kind of bread would you like? Mayo or mustard? Or both? Each perfect triangle stuffed with promise. She hated it when her customers took their first bites. She would go back to school and eventually graduate, take courses in ECE. Perhaps she would travel. But then, leaning forward one day at an intersection, she almost tipped over into the road along which a truck was barreling and felt a hand grab her and pull her back. *Don't do it.* I wasn't trying, she muttered. I'm in a hurry. The man had no hair. Dressed all in black, wearing black canvas boots, his white head was criss-crossed with thorns, roses, vines. On closer inspection he was also old; forty at least. *Are you on something? Can I talk you down?* They ended up in a smelly second-hand bookstore where Susan bought a copy of *Anna Karenina*. They then went to a deli, where they tasted samples of paper-thin sliced German salami. Held up to the light, it was flesh, stained glass.

Con was an ex, an ex-con, with a son and a record. His body was entirely covered in tattoos. Susan found them disorienting yet inviting, never quite sure which limb, which joint was which. He drove her around on his Harley and they went camping, waking up in bad moods with gritty mouths only to unzip a flap and walk into paradise. Once Susan took a shit and stood up into mist so thick she was lost, just she and her feces surrounded by white and it was Con's voice that pulled her back into air again, stepping slowly over rocks and ground squirrels into the clearing where her pack sat, patient and solid, like a part of her she'd abandoned rather cruelly and now regarded with unconditional joy.

Con proposed. Susan guffawed. I'm practically the same age as your son. But she moved in anyway. Anything seemed better than living with her parents. She told them she was moving in with a girlfriend. Surprisingly they didn't react. Perhaps they were disappointed. They always seemed to feel that way. She knew they'd been disappointed when they went to Hawaii. The beaches weren't white enough, the sun not hot enough. The contentment they had radiated was merely relief. As she walked out the door, Susan wished for a moment they would stop her. Perhaps if they tried to restrain her she would fall in love with them: it could happen, technically, it wasn't too late. All kinds of people adored their parents, especially older people who had left home. Meanwhile Con was fun, a reasonable stand-in. He meditated daily, a habit he had acquired in the slammer and soon she found herself joining in. Sitting beside him in silence was maddening, yet she could not help it. His knees clicked as he sat down on his zafu. His nose whistled, his breath slowed and she wondered what the hell he could possibly be thinking about. A siren rose and fell, turned into a fly which morphed into her mother then Ally McBeal. Her head jerked. A pig snorted. Was that her? Opening her eyes she regarded Con's clock, the hands on which appeared to be going backwards. Who was this man who had grabbed her and called her to him? He was an ex-punk. He played guitar. He educated youth about sobriety, bought groceries for little old ladies and in between worked out at the gym. And now she was with him, he seemed so young, like a man whose body ages and mind regresses, his enthusiasm for life borderline ludicrous. He saw his son twice a week and lived in a tiny apartment filled with action figures. Next to him she felt very old, her months with Anton a fascinating secret she would not share even if he tortured her, which clearly he wouldn't. He had other things on his mind.

Yet she did love his head. It was prickly, flabby and she could pinch a yellowing handful between her fingers, a handful that might contain roses or thorns. He shaved it every other day and when he did she liked to dab on the shaving cream, scrape the razor over its stubble and watch his blood rushing up to the surface and this reminded her for some reason of Anton, who never shaved, never grew facial hair, only worshipped the great cloud that sat on his head. One day she took Con down there, to the walkup where she had lived, pretended she was lost. They were on their way to a movie downtown and on an impulse she had suggested they walk. Off the bike, he seemed uncertain. She led, walking briskly between junkies, considered running, seeing how fast he could go, but in the end needed him behind her, a tall, striped presence like a beacon. Anton was nowhere. The walkup had yellow tickertape around it and police strode up and down looking purposeful. There had been a crime: that much was certain, but what had been done to whom no one knew.

Freak Waves

As with any cataclysmic event, there are the days before, and the days after, days of ordinary clement or inclement weather which blur into a general impression of grey, slashed apart by glory. Right now, sun is lying in strips on Ray's desktop, cut into neat pieces by the half-open blind.

On August 1, 1869, in California, a cow fell from the sky in butchered pieces: a rib here, a tube of intestine there. In July 2001, a rain of blood fell on the Indian state of Kerala, preceded by thunder, a flash of light, and leaves graying and shriveling off the trees. The blood was later found to be a kind of fungus. Yellow, black and green rains were also seen. On July 9, 1958, the largest freak wave ever recorded swept an Alaskan fisherman and his wife out into the ocean. The wave's initial height was 1,700 feet, over 50m higher than the Empire State building. Four years later the fisherman, Bill Swanson, revisited the site of Lituya Bay only to die of a massive heart attack just at the entrance.

Perhaps there is a special part of heaven reserved for those who perish through acts of God. Possibly Lorraine Smith is there, chatting wittily. On March 24, 2010 (it is now May 27) Lorraine went missing from an ancient burial site somewhere off the north-west coast of Maui. All Ray understands is that one minute she was there, admiring a sunset, and the next she was gone, the world closing up behind her, a wound in calm blue water quickly healed.

There's a stirring of breeze through the stale rooms of his apartment, the whistles of chickadees ready for tea outside.

Ray does not consider himself creative. Nor has beauty ever been his domain. No, he's always the workhorse, a draftsman for hire, whereas Lorraine despises effort, considers it cheating. She laughs at anyone who asks how she makes money, never applies for grants and loathes teaching. She also never visibly prepares for a show. Yet every day she produces and produces, the work piling up until it just has to be sold otherwise they would have to rent another apartment. Right now, for example, a stack of finished canvasses are turned like resting actors towards the wall.

Did you know the largest wave marine architects are required to prepare for is fifteen metres high? Under normal conditions, this is the largest wave an oceangoing vessel is likely to encounter. However, science has recently uncovered the phenomenon of freak waves, up to thirty metres in height, which can and do appear literally out of nowhere.

The week before she left, she seemed excited. The new lines on her face were complex, urgent, like hieroglyphics he should have learned how to read. Ray said he had decided to decline her offer. Lorraine seemed shocked and said she would go anyway. There was someone she'd met, someone she wanted to spend time with. He told her to be careful, and that was all.

Rogue waves seem to occur in deep water or where a number of physical factors such as strong winds and fast currents converge. This may have a focusing effect, which can cause a number of waves to join together. The Draupner wave, a single giant wave measured on New Year's Day 1995, finally confirmed the existence of freak waves, which had previously been considered near-mythical.

Lorraine was alone when she disappeared. This irks him particularly for, unlike Ray, she thought nothing of sleeping outdoors in the city, or asking a total stranger to hold her purse. And although she struggled with time, she trusted people. He thinks maybe she trusted people too much.

Last weekend he phoned her parents. Ross answered. He sounded pleased to hear from Ray, but then Gwen snatched the phone and told him not to call back.

He can't imagine what they must both be going through.

Let alone what he himself is going through.

He has started collecting her skin cells and her hair.

"Where are you, Lorraine?"

The fan whirls round.

A panic fills him: what if she's still alive, drifting around in the middle of the Pacific? Ray goes out onto the balcony, breathes in gouts of warm fresh air. After a while an old friend reappears.

"Hi, Ray. Got anything for me?"

"It's all out there in the box."

Ray watches George help himself to the newly washed bottles, one of which held a particularly good Pinot Noir. Behind him a car creeps by, boom box thumping. Out beyond the alley, between the high-rises, the park's trees rise up shivering dryly.

Even Lorraine said this was a beautiful city. Soon the kids will be out screeching in the fountains, their section of the park separate from that of the junkies, who sit and trade and bicker unimpeded while mothers flash them glances from beside the swings. Soon someone will lay out a spread of goods to sell by the sidewalk, and either the spiritual healers or the African drummers will set up beside them. Meanwhile Ray will spend his day inside. He does not like to mingle, especially in summer. If he goes out at all, it will be very late. Even the sick and ill look good in the half-light, offering up empty coffee cups, half-carved masks.

Leaning out across the morning, he watches motionless shrubs and bushes solidify, a diving swallow turn to stone in mid-flight. The herb pots Lorraine planted are as dry as sandpits. Soon all he'll have will be an empty balcony, its peeling boards pitted with avian corpses. A hairbrush picked clean of evidence and excuses, a roomful of paint he has no idea how to use.

He goes back inside to check the weather. There must be rain falling softly somewhere. Prince Rupert, BC: eight degrees, light rain; Maui country club: thirty degrees and windy; McMurdo, Antarctica: minus thirty-two and snow.

Scientists are divided over whether or not global warming has increased the incidence of these seemingly unprovoked tsunamis. Statistics certainly point to their increased frequency. However this could also be due to more diligent reporting. The fact is, many ships sink without a trace.

When the person she wanted to be with phoned at midnight, he picked up, of course, hoping it was her. Instead, what he got was a man his own age weeping. Lorraine had not returned. A wave had swept up, sucked a rental car clean off the highway. Ray's wife was considered missing, drowned.

Some people think if they go south their lives will get easier. But they're wrong, aren't they. An aseptic, utterly infertile environment: that's what the south really is if you just go far enough, past Cape Horn and Tierra del Fuego, right down deep to the very bottom of the world.

One day soon he will have to return the baby blanket Ross and Gwen passed on for the two of them to use. At forty-two, Lorraine was still in the running. Gwen was forty-four when Lorraine was adopted, a dark-eyed foundling whose delivery to the steps of their church was Ray's wife's confounding. *Is anyone no one?* She wasn't what they wanted, but she did try.

Miracles do happen. In July 2009 one resident of Japan's Ishikawa Prefecture discovered thirteen dead carp around his car, while another heard a strange noise in a nearby parking lot and discovered the lot covered with hundreds of tadpoles. And in 1947 a chicken lived for a year after its head was cut off because somehow the farmer missed its brain stem and jugular.

How long must he wait? The man in Hawaii has urged him to come and visit, but Ray has declined. Trust your instincts, Lor, believe no rumors. If things seem bad, they are probably much worse. Recently, two satellites surveyed the oceans, and during a three-week period detected ten 25-metre waves. Ray's wife has been missing for sixty-four days now. These may be facts, but they do not help. What matters is that Lorraine no longer loved him. She did not want to be with him anymore.

A woman's leg in a shoe falls past his window. Unaware, Ray takes a pair of scissors, selects a graphic sketch to take it out on. Cutting through delusion is laborious, especially when you have inadequate tools. Ray never showed this one to Lorraine, in part because he did not think it was good enough. Now he wishes he had, but it's too late, isn't it. All evidence and fact, Ray flexes his knuckles: the flash of her eyes, the jut of her hip, some dappled blue chaise-longue into which she collapses, curled naked and alone and with her back to him. Where are you, now? Body parts continue to fly past. Can something more be made out of something less? Ray reassembles Lor's face momentarily. Lorraine would enjoy this game. She is enjoying it, alone again on the far side of a wall of water, waiting for him to join her, to have a heart attack – but he can't, can he, because she once hurt his pride, near cut his head off, his cry the cosmic cluck of a headless chicken, ridiculous yet continuing to be.

Salt and Clay

WHILE MATT FUCKS HER in uneven jerks, Shelley gazes out through the bedroom window, transforms herself distantly into Whitton Flash: its shoreline all that remains of the flooded salt mine, a shard of sunlit water through windblown trees. Or perhaps crystal: the Flash's calm is potent, but artificial, dispersed by the hacking coughs of retired miners. Shelley's father worked there. It was a tough job.

"Salt gets in their cuts, you know, while they're working. Plus the salt air eats away their skin."

As Matt works and sweats, she remembers this conversation. Her mother had been seated before her lukewarm gas fire, the requisite glass of sherry in hand. Matt had been fixing the fake tree in the hallway while Shelley nursed her widowed mother's bubble bath, waiting for an appropriate moment to pass it on.

"Walks up and down those stairs in his big boots, moaning and groaning. You'd think he still lived here." Her mother was describing her father, who seemed to have returned to his wife as a ghost. "It's not like we parted on good terms. I mean, you know how it was, Shel: we hadn't seen each other for years."

"Are you sure you're not imagining it?"

"Yes, dear."

Afraid to probe further, Shelley had swiftly produced the gift-wrapped bubble bath. After all, it wasn't like her mother to see things, least of all Shelley's father, whom she loathed. Boots caked with clay, dirt-stiffened trousers: all Shelley could conjure of the man who left when she was five seemed peripheral. Her memories of Uncle Jed, the man Shelley's mother had lived with for three years afterward, were equally disorienting: sticky white fingers stinking of nicotine, a long lock of red hair plastered across a freckled, bald head.

"It hurts, you know, when he scares me. I feel it right here." Ignoring the gift, her mother had clutched at her thin chest, laden with cheap beads. "He always said he wanted to cause me agony; as if I wasn't the one who'd given birth."

Matt comes now and Shelley rolls over onto her side. She knows she will never give birth. Too much of a coward, or at least that's what she'll say when the time comes. For now she has to figure out how to leave him. Yet, like the track between here and Whitton Flash, that path is treacherous.

"That rapist's up for parole today," says Matt, wiping his cock off.

"Who?" asks Shelley, wrapping a towel round her waist.

"The bloke who murdered all those whores." Matt gestures mutely as if supporting an invisible corpse with his hands.

"Oh yeah," says Shelley. It's strange, she reflects, how resilient names are. Even now, after all that has happened, "Jackie" remains pungent, spiky with potential mischief, reminiscent of sherbet, the explosive, yellow kind you could suck through a straw.

"I'm going for a walk," she says quietly. If she leaves now, she will have two hours of safety. The track is peopled by ramblers until after well dark. She pulls on her track suit bottoms, lunges for a T-shirt, but before she can reach the staircase he has her by the wrists.

"I'm worried about you," he says, pushing her backwards until their soft mattress collapses her knees. "Don't forget there's a nutcase about." He lets go of her, snatches her keys up. "Keep the chain on the front door. I'll be back."

Before she can protest he has slammed the front door, its frost-patterned glass reverberating. As revenge, she decides to take a nip of rum, goes downstairs and unearths it, fills a plastic tumbler. The sickly taste fascinates, like that of the opiate-spiked cough medicine she drank as a youngster. She pours another tumbler and another, and soon it's as if the semi is subsiding, her legs are melting. It's entirely possible: the mine is gone, but the ground, unforgiving, still plays tricks. Salt crystals rise to its surface. Vegetable plots sink another inch each year. Sprawled on the kitchen floor, she gives in to nostalgia. When Jackie was alive they would play in the marl pits, making clay ovens or pretending one or other was the Salt Mine Man, a bald white ogre, his face and hands eaten away, who lurched like Frankenstein's monster towards children, desperate to slake his thirst on the sweet blood of girls.

"Who's afraid of the Salt Mine Man?"

"Not me!"

Whoever tripped and fell had been killed by the ogre. Whoever made it to the sycamore tree had survived.

Shelley's dad worked in the mine until it closed. Then he got a job in a paint factory. A big, strong man, his presence, she supposes, was a night-light's, thinning the dark, for after he left, when she was five, a hole opened up in her universe, out of which fear seeped. Soon its shimmer blurred everything in her path: the front gate, the street, the station, the railway line, the main road, the rest of the village, even the small farms that lay beyond. All that remained steady was the

unknown – adjacent villages, distant cities, foreign place-
names the atlas yielded up: Pennsylvania, Guadalajara, Niger.
By the time Shelley was twelve she had lived many lives in
other places: brief, bright existences fuelled often by a single
word.

By the time she reached fourteen she was spending most of
her spare time in bed. *Tasmania,* she would think to herself,
savouring each syllable. *Boston, Massachusetts. Northallerton.
Sierra Leone.* One day her mother walked up and upended a
saucepan of dirty dishwater all over her.

"I've been calling you for hours!" she yelled as Shelley rose
up spluttering, picking bits of pork fat out of her hair.
"Bloody well come and dry up!"

The duvet got washed but always retained a greasy spot up
near the top. A few days later, acknowledging she couldn't
stay home forever, at least not beyond sixteen, Shelley
decided – partly to spite her mother – that it was time she
defected to the other side, time to make a pact with her own
private devil. In return for permission to live, she would seek
danger out, walk towards terror without thinking. Find what
it was that scared her before it found her.

Paul Clay, for example, who lived with his brother and sister in the next street: ten years Shelley's senior and rumoured
to have killed a man, or that's what Jackie had implied. Jackie
should know: she'd been to one of his parties. Ever since Shelley had reached puberty she'd felt Paul's eyes on her, evaluat-
ing her legs, her breasts, her hair. It was obvious what would
happen, sooner or later. The Yorkshire Ripper's crimes were
all over the news. So before he could rape her at knife-point
then slash her into tiny little pieces, she marched up to his
door, knocked hard, got invited in.

While Shelley perched on the settee, Paul closed the curtains, ostensibly to protect he and Shelley from the sun. The

living room carpet was littered with plastic doll parts, dirty dinner plates, empty Heineken cans.

"'Scuse the mess, only my sister Deirdre's away at the moment."

Paul's arms were blue with tattoos. Even at this distance Shelley could make out words amongst the pictures: "Satan" across one bicep; stacked across the other, "Juliet" and "Mam."

"Can I get you anything?"

Shelley shook her head. Her legs were crossed at the ankle in an attempt to look elegant, like that skinny Sue Ellen from off TV, but her hands were trembling. So before she could chicken out, she began unbuttoning the blouse beneath her dark brown cardigan. After all, she'd told Paul at the door she had something to show him.

Suddenly, without warning, they were kissing. She'd never felt someone's tongue rub against her own before. Whether or not she enjoyed it was immaterial. Something inside her was worth seeking, mining for. As Paul's hands clawed at the waistband of her knickers, Shelley flinched, took a deep breath then leaned back in.

By the time she got home it was time for tea: fishcakes and oven chips. Paul had almost screwed her but the phone rang; it was an important call. Admittedly, she'd felt relieved when he told her to go – feeling his engorged penis push up against her had been danger enough.

The second time Shelley pressed the doorbell Paul answered the door in his dressing-gown. It was black terry toweling with dark orange piping. Instead of ushering her into the lounge this time, he took her by the hand and steered her up the steep stairs to his room.

"Lie down," he ordered. A Rod Stewart record was playing on the hi-fi next door – she could hear it through the padded vinyl headboard. When Paul slipped his dressing-gown off and turned round, a large green dragon was visible traversing his buttocks.

"Did you really go to prison?" asked Shelley, but got no answer. Paul was on top of her already, fingers in her bra, mouth coming down on her mouth.

"I shouldn't have done that," said Paul afterwards. "You're a witch, you are, mind," he added, "a real prick-tease."

Shelley forced a laugh. She felt quite sore. Was that sex, she asked herself. Suddenly she felt embarrassed about her uneven-sized tits and pulled the burgundy cotton sheets far up. Paul's penis was limp now, beneath his hairy belly. As he rolled over and stood up he seemed nervous, alien; almost old.

"Listen, don't come here again," he said. "You're a nice lass and everything, but, well, you know what I mean don't you, it's not right." He was standing by the bed, his arms folded, distant. As Shelley flicked her eyes around the room she caught sight of a Swiss army knife partially unfolded, exposed beneath a broken-spined paperback.

Paul threw something at her from across the landing. She ducked, petrified. Black corduroy drainpipes, pink polo-neck jumper, fringed purse: it was her special outfit. As the shower started in the bathroom she let herself out.

Jacqueline Titania Gormley. Thin and dark, at nine she claimed she was an exiled Russian princess, at eleven swore on the Bible she was related to Gandhi. Her middle name came from Shakespeare because both her mother and father were film stars – or wanted to be, once, before they got married. In reality they owned a fleet of ice cream vans. At sixteen she was found dead in a cornfield, strangled with her own black studded belt.

When Shelley told Jackie about sleeping with Paul, Jackie didn't seem impressed. Instead she just took another drag on her menthol cigarette and went on to describe her cousin Robert's tattoo. Robert was twenty-five and worked on an oil rig.

"It's a Chinese dragon: bright red. And get this: when he comes, like, it curls around his thigh and licks his dick."

Robert, Jackie went on to say, had screwed her twice a year since she turned eight. "Christmas and Easter." Those were the only times that he got leave.

There was an awkward pause then the two of them cracked up and Shelley poured yet more wine into Jackie's mouth.

After that, Shelley felt oddly safer, as if some burden of secrecy had been lifted. She and Jackie had known each other for years, yet only now were they real best mates.

Jackie and Shelley stuffing themselves with Smarties; the two of them in hot-pants, playing outside: British Bulldog, True Dare Kiss Command or Promise: the two of them had always been close. There were other children in the Row. Matthew Harris, for example, who spent his life rehearsing headers for the day he would represent England at the World Cup. Matthew's best friend, Gary Vickers, who scooped up spawn from the stagnant pond each spring and stored it in glass jars until it hatched. Gary Vickers, who said he couldn't wait until he grew up and became a fireman. How could he possibly know what he wanted, thought Shelley, who only ever wanted to go backwards, to regress to babyhood and then onto oblivion. In her dreams, Gary's frogs leapt backwards, reabsorbed their legs then shrank back down into dots, until, with consummate tenderness,

Gary-in-the-dream opened his fingers and released the
frogspawn back into the pond.

Two older girls, Tracey Jones and Mandy Entwistle, lived
at numbers seven and two respectively. Until both got jobs
they giggled constantly, their caved-in shoulders shuddering
with mirth which from a distance could easily be mistaken for
grief.

Tracey now worked for a bank in Didsbury while Mandy
waited tables at the Salt Museum. Both smiled politely but
rarely giggled, unless they had each had several pints, and
even then it was a tired, adult laugh.

Shelley knew them all as if they were family, but Jackie was
now the only one she trusted. At school the others thought
Shelley was frigid, because she wore lace-ups and ignored
boys. Only Jackie knew of Shelley's turmoil, the fear that
drew her to adulthood, then pushed her back.

It was Tracey and Mandy together who found Jackie's
body. Or rather, her clothes: navy blue pencil skirt ripped up
the side, red nylon bomber jacket, pair of black patent stiletto
heels. There was a watch as well, but it was all crushed, said
Mandy. You couldn't even read the Mickey Mouse face. The
clothes were bundled up in a bin bag and had been stuffed
into a lidded rubbish bin just off the motorway. By the time
the clothes were found, Jackie had been missing for almost
five days.

The following weekend a pensioner with a metal detec-
tor discovered something interesting in a field. It was late
April, wet and lush, the hedgerows filled with coltsfoot,
celandine. The small hard object was not, as it turned out,
a Viking shield stud, but one of Jackie's gold-filled teeth.
Her uncle was a dentist and had done them for her, two
lower molars rotted out by penny chews. Thin as she was,
Jackie always liked her sweets. The tooth led to a

bloodstained rock, the bloodstained rock to a cold blue hand, and the cold blue hand, via a stiff, crooked arm, to a purple face. Jackie Gormley's body was buried in a shallow grave, a hundred yards from where the Salt Mine Man had often stalked her.

By the time Shelley got down there, the field had been sealed off with ticker tape. Cars were parked up and down the lane. Policemen in reflective vests were shooing away journalists. Off to one side a camera crew from Look Northwest had suspended a huge furry boom above the heads of onlookers, while a woman with blonde hair spoke into an orange-tipped mike.

Young girl's clothing – tragedy – decomposing: fragments of reportage broke off and stuck in Shelley's chest, causing her to gasp for air.

"Are you all right, love?" A concerned policewoman strode swiftly toward her. Behind the woman a bald white ogre was also visible, rising up from the black plastic sheeting the police had spread across the churned-up grass.

After Jackie's death the Row became very quiet. Even though the police suspected her attacker was a serial killer from Lancashire who had been apprehended the following week, no one felt safe outdoors all summer long. In the pub, Mandy and Tracey, who still went everywhere together, were quizzed time and again.

Meanwhile, after a brief period of mourning, Jackie's parents sold their ice cream business and decided to move up to Glasgow to start a new life. The week before they left they sold their soft-serve cones at a massive discount.

"Might as well use these up," smiled Mrs. Gormley tautly, elegant in a black velour tracksuit. "Everything tastes of salt here anyway."

After they had left, Shelley discovered she hated ice cream. After school, instead of taking the bus into town, she went straight home to lie on her bed. Then around five, just before her mother got home from the off-licence, she would slip out the back door wrapped in her donkey jacket and run as fast as she could in whatever direction until she reached a place where she felt unseen.

Why did this happen? She would ask, scribbling her question on a torn-off piece of paper and rolling it into a pellet. *Who did this to you? Where are you?* Sometimes the pellets were flicked over her left shoulder, which meant Jackie was in hell, other times her right shoulder, which meant she was in heaven. Still others she folded the paper three times and posted it into a slot between two railings, which meant Jackie was out there, somewhere. All of this happened in the thin air of the motorway overpass, the high concrete bridge beneath which cars sped on their way to the future. Shelley found herself up there more and more often, seeking refuge from the dead quiet of the fields.

At the end of June she left school, in August accepted a job in the village bakery. Mandy Entwistle's mum, who worked there too, had taken pity on her – it was known throughout the village that Shelley had drunk too much at the end-of-term disco and ended up passing out on the dance floor. A stress reaction, and entirely out of character, Miss Freer, the new Deputy Head, had politely insisted, after driving Shelley home. On the doorstep Shelley's mother apologized profusely. It was only after the front door slammed that she gave her daughter what she truly deserved.

As the belt uncoiled with a crack across her backside, Shelley felt both intense pain and relief. Three inches taller than her mother, she could have wrestled her to the ground yet there was something comforting about the beating. Each slap across her flesh stung brightly, justly. For she *had* been naughty: she should have taken better care of Jackie, should have been a more protective friend.

I really, really should have stopped her, thought Shelley again, six weeks later, leaning crazily over the parapet. Beneath her, polished cars zoomed, herself the apex of the arc their sound made, its highest point before the low 'whoosh' south. *I should have told her not to be so daft.*

Jackie's voice came back to her suddenly, describing some fat man she'd met in the station bar. He'd bought her three cherry brandies and a snakebite then paid her twenty quid for oral sex. Jackie was triumphant.

"Is he married?" Shelley remembered asking. They'd just caught the Yorkshire Ripper, an ordinary man with a beard who came home clean to his wife, after killing women, for dinner. Jackie had said no but that she had a date that night. "With cherry brandy?"

"No, different bloke, I'll tell you later." But there was no later.

And now there was no Jackie. Only boring fatherless Shelley, who'd stayed home that night and watched TV.

I should have stopped her. Instead she could stop herself now. She could jump. Would that atone? The thought of dying made her eyes water, all the headlights merge into taillights and a big fist rise up in her chest. The fist clamped down, pinned her to the railings. Between them she thought she discerned an elsewhere, a parallel world where no one made mistakes. She wanted to go there. But just as she was shifting her weight Paul Clay's brother Mike drove by on his motorbike. He seemed to be heading for the chemical plant, a grey boxlike building at the edge of the village. But catching sight of Shelley he swerved then parked.

"Hey up! What the hell do you think you're doing?"

One minute she was about to die, the next Mike Clay was loping towards her, an alien spaceman in leathers and cherry Docs.

"What's it to you?"

"I thought you were going to, you know –"

Her heart lurched. She leaned back, feigned nonchalance. The Clays had moved a few months after she had slept with Paul, and she hadn't seen any of them for years.

"Well, anyroad, if you're all right –"

"Yes, I am, I'm fine, honestly."

Mike's eyes darted around her. What did he know? "I'm late for work –" He scratched his head. "Are you coming?" When she didn't move he knelt down, put his face close, the tenderness in his voice spiked with malice. "Come on now, don't be stupid."

"Okay." Shelley let go of the motorway overpass parapet and walked with him back to the village road. A few minutes later, as the two awkwardly prepared to part ways, Michael's eyes caught hers and the look in them, nonchalant yet titillated, turned inside her body like a blade. One she was no longer standing at the edge of, but could feel quite distinctly, cutting through.

"See you," he said, slapping her hard on the shoulder.

"Yeah," she replied. So it was life, then. "Yeah, Mike, see you around."

Shelley met Mike for a drink the following weekend. Like his brother, Mike smoked incessantly, lighting one cigarette from another, and she found almost nothing to say, except "yes" when he asked her if she wanted to go for a walk. It was a humid evening, patches of tarmac sticky from the afternoon heat. They walked past the school, its windows full of last term's paintings, through the new estate to the marshes, where back gardens edged onto fields. Shelley ran her hand up the back of Mike's stubbly head. Instead of reciprocating, Mike grabbed her arm and held her in a half nelson.

"I've heard about you," he grinned. Then he ran off.

What did he know? Folding her arms in front of her chest as a discreet way of relieving the pain, Shelley reluctantly followed. Soon she was sprinting, heels in hand, chasing Mike as he dodged kids and pensioners to disappear down an alley then in through the back door of a house.

What was he doing here? 24 Elm Tree Close was an old brick semi-detached that hadn't been lived in for years. Scheduled for demolition after a terrible fire, its smoke-stained front loomed oddly dark between the shiny semis on either side. Once inside, Shelley was amazed to see new paper on the walls, a mismatched three piece suite arranged around the gas fire. On closer inspection, the paper was pages from dirty magazines and the red plush settee pocked with cigarette burns, but the place was definitely inhabited.

"Is this where you live now?"

"Fuck off," said Mike. "It's my brother's mate's house. Lee the Lad's." Judging from the décor, which was mostly centerfolds interspersed with newspaper clippings, Lee the Looney would have been more like it. Was it someone Paul had met in jail? As if in reply, Mike reached into his pocket and pulled out a spliff. After taking a long drag he handed it to Shelley.

"Nice place," she said, trying not to cough. Normally it would have scared her, breaking into a well-known haunted house. But since the day on the overpass nothing registered, as if she had truly died then, or at least gone to sleep. She handed the joint back to Mike, who cupped his hands around it, breathed deeply.

"Where is he then, this Lee?"

143

"In hell," said Mike, pointing his fingers up like devil horns.

"Shouldn't that be the other way?" Shelley pointed downward. Mike grinned, took her hand and led her up the shattered staircase, opened the door on a room that was clearly once a child's. Grimy flaps of Mickey Mouse wallpaper were patched together with black plastic bin bags, a filthy orange rug over one wall. Crushed beer cans, overflowing ash trays and a cracked water pipe lay like bomb detritus beneath an opaque window, two single mattresses covered by stained blue sheets closer to the door.

"Fancy a screw?" Mike's grin was manic, desperate. Shelley decided not to wonder why.

"Okay," she said, slipping off her blouse. What the hell. It was easy enough to blur things in her mind. Perhaps the room was theirs, in a foreign hotel, the cries of kids outside conversation from the patio. She was just about to decide on a location when Mike pushed her down hard from behind. She grabbed his arms and they danced strangely for a moment before he rolled her over, tugged at her skirt, sending one of its red buttons flying. She rolled back over, yanked off her knickers.

In and out, in and out – Mike was suddenly doing press-ups over her. Glancing down she noticed her ribs pushing back up at him through her skin.

"Oh, oh," she faked. Each time he thrust she tried to resist, arching her neck and raising her pelvis as if she were orgasming but there wasn't enough room, she was pressed to the wall, and anyway Mike didn't care. His eyes remained closed. He came quickly. Afterwards he blew smoke rings, said she was a good fuck, not bad at all for a prude.

"I'm not a fucking prude!" She was angry now, pissed off and sore. While Mike struggled to light his roach she grabbed one of his Camels, started pulling it apart on the dirty sheet. Brown flakes of tobacco accumulated like sawdust, rabbit litter.

"Was your brother really a murderer?"

Mike snorted, coughed, his face all sweaty suddenly, his body shuddering a silent mirthless laugh.

Shelley turned away. The buzz from the hash now wearing off, she was feeling hungry. Nothing to eat here: that much was obvious. Just filth and grime – a red lace-up shoe, Mike's stinking socks, someone else's used condoms wadded together in a yellowish heap, like snotty hankies. I want to go home, she thought to herself, her inner voice whiny. Instead she stood up and stumbled across to the window, wondering if the kid who once lived here could see her, was peeking out from between flaps of sooty wallpaper this very minute, desperate for her to recognize him but she could not.

Looking at Mike shivering oddly on the mattress she snapped, suddenly grabbed her skirt off the floor and started whipping him with it, lifting it high over her head then down, down. The remaining plastic buttons clattered against him. Next she went down on her knees, grabbed his arm and sunk her painted nails into it, growling, not knowing what was happening. Her hands gripped his flesh as if to crush it. Her jaw clenched. She lunged and bit him on the chest but it was a small bite, hair and skin and her head knocked back so hard she lost consciousness, the dark nothing a respite that refreshed but it was too late, Mike was on top of her, holding her down, his spit stinging her eye as he uncoiled his belt from his jeans, hooked it round her neck.

"You're going to die." His voice was hoarse with intent. She felt the buckle press in, cold and unyielding against her esophagus, her own skin burning, wondered if Jackie had felt

Something About the Animal

this when she died. Except it wasn't summer then but spring. Shelley's breath came in jagged gasps. Mike yanked the belt as if to snap her neck. She couldn't see. She *was* going to die. Then she heard someone whistle and Mike let go, left her drowning in air while he exited the bedroom to stand outside on the landing, alone.

"Lee!"

"Who's this?" A fat man in a green T-shirt leaned towards her. His pale face was slick with sweat or oil. "Caught you in the act, did I?" Mike muttered a response nearby. Before she could work out what it was the fat man grabbed her chin, tilted her face towards him. "Nice." Then he let go.

Mike was in the corner shooting up, his belt now a tourniquet. She watched fascinated as he palpated for veins then stuck the needle in swiftly, one casual jab, as if he were puncturing a balloon. Why hadn't she seen any scars? He looked like a saint, some martyr or other from the Middle Ages: face rapt, skin translucent as parchment. Perhaps she had thought his track marks were insect bites.

Free to go, or so she thought, Lee trapped her on the landing. While he spoke, Shelley memorized his lips, recalled an illustration from fifth-form History – "instruments of torture" – a line drawing of an Inquisitor surrounded by whips, flails, to which someone had added a flaccid penis.

"I know you," he was saying quietly. "You were her friend." Shelley bent down, slipped under his arm, descended the stairs and closed the door of the haunted house behind her. Her neck ached; her throat was raw and tender. She had left her sandals behind, they had been brand new, and her clothes hung away from her absurdly, as if they had been purchased for someone else.

146

Matthew Harris had never made it to the World Cup, but was a successful plumber who worked hard and had respectable vices: he drank at the George and Dragon on Fridays and Saturdays, played football every other weekend. For their honeymoon, three years to the day since she screwed Mike Clay, they had traveled to Ibiza, where Shelley ate octopus for the first time and developed second-degree burns across her shoulders. Finally she had arrived somewhere real; a destination you could look up in an atlas. Day after day, while Matt drank, she lounged on a big purple towel, deliberately forgetting to apply suntan lotion, staring out across the head-filled sea. Since the fat man Lee had touched her, all she wanted to do was rest.

After two weeks of bliss they flew home via Stansted and life continued as per usual, except they were now living together. In their spare time, Shelley cooked and cleaned and plumped cushions, Matt worked on his van and brewed beer. Every other night he made love to her with workmanlike precision. Shelley avoided thoughts of strangulation, although after a year of marriage, Matt, still tender in public, had begun to rough her up a bit in private, leave bruises on her upper arms. Meanwhile, on certain weekends, lining up for scrag end at the butcher's or purchasing cut-price custard tarts at the corner bakery, she saw Mike Clay, passing in the street, and tried to catch a glimpse of his inner arms. Yet even in summer they were covered up, and he in turn looked through her, as if she were air. It was hard for her to review the hours they had spent together. Details receded and were replaced by sense impressions: hands attached to a face; a voice intoning threats. In the same way she avoided the facts of her marriage. Matt's eyes: were they blue or grey? Why did he never seem to blink?

Meanwhile Jackie's murder remained unsolved and the field where her body had been discovered disappeared beneath a brand new housing estate: the Clyde, all instant grass, its pristine lanes and cul-de-sacs named poetically after Scottish islands – Arran Close, Skye Avenue, Iona Drive – which filled up rapidly with local families, all eager to live in homes with zero subsidence, on streets without reputations, either good or bad. The second summer after they were married, Matt suggested they move in too. They could barely afford to, but the Clyde semis were selling fast, and their tiny flat over Lipton's stank of rotting vegetables. That Christmas Matt and Shelley moved into a brand new paint-smelling semi, number sixteen, Arran Close.

They found the Irish miners in February, in the second year of their marriage, when things had changed a little. Shelley had already been to Accident and Emergency twice since New Year's. The second time a nurse took her aside and slipped her the phone number of a hotline, but Shelley just smiled and explained once again, in simpler words this time, that her cracked rib was the result of an accident.

The gash in her thigh that had happened next wasn't Matt's fault at all but the result of her own weird experiment: one night while he was down the pub she had remembered Jackie and her becoming blood sisters that previous July down by the river and suddenly needed to know if blood was indeed hot, for that was how she recalled it, a sweet, warm river of shock along her best friend's arm.

"What are you doing?" asked Matt when he stumbled in and saw her unwrapping the razor blade, legs open and bare before the blaring television.

"Shaving," she replied.

"Don't be ridiculous." He took the blade away then grasped her shoulders. "You mad cunt." At first he cradled her tightly. She supposed she'd given him reason to be attentive. But by the time the news crews once again reached the village, this time to report on older bones, he'd almost convinced her violence was a form of care.

"Slapping," he announced, while she felt her skull bounce off the kitchen cabinets, "is a cure for hysteria. Didn't you know that?" Mike Clay had never left, just hidden. Matt Harris cradled the same dark.

Shelley rushed home from the village that day feeling nothing, fresh lamb chops dripping blood through the base of her bag. The council had decided the haunted house was a hotbed of drug use, and moved in to demolish. The walls crumbled like pastry as the wrecking ball hit them, and soon the foundations were exposed, a cracked square of cement that split in two to reveal old salt pans, collapsed workings no one had known were there. The overeager developer found even more. "Bodies of Irish found in startling condition" read the Tribune's headline. In fact the workers' putrid flesh was pitted with old wounds, preserved by the very substance that caused them.

As the archeologists examined them it became apparent that three of the bodies were recent: very recent. It was then discovered a tunnel had existed, through which the old workings could be accessed from the demolished house.

Shelley knew nothing of this until weeks later. This all changed on a sunny Friday in April after Matt pointed his fork at the TV screen.

"Jesus Christ, I know him." A pea fell off then a dollop of shepherd's pie. Shelley tried not to panic, but grease marks on the tablecloth were exactly the kind of thing that set him off. To calm herself she looked away and caught the fat man's face flashed across the screen above an image of 24 Elm Tree

Close as it was before the demolition. *Northallerton, Sierra Leone, Guadalajara.* Jacqueline Titania Gormley. What if she couldn't get the grease mark out?

"He's a fucking murderer!"

"Murdered," echoed the female newsreader, primly. Three grainy photographs hovered behind her. One of them was of Jackie. "In other news ..." Matt fumbled for a second, pressed the remote.

"Fucking hell! I knew her. Didn't you?" He reached for his cigarettes, the ashtray. "Amazing what they can do these days, DNA and all that."

The local news replaced by sports, Shelley stared open-mouthed at men running around in knee socks, wondered if Matt could read her mind the way she could read the score: Wolves 3, Luton 6. Seven and a half minutes until penalty. Could he see the red lace-up shoe, the Mickey Mouse wallpaper, read the words *Fancy a screw* written right through her in hot pink crystallized sugar, as if she were a stick of Blackpool rock?

That shoe was Jackie's. Of course it was. Jackie always tucked a pair of flats in her bag, along with a tube of spermicide, breath mints, the glittery make-up kit she got from the chemist's, enough money for a taxi home. For all her stupidity, Jackie kept her wits about her. In her mind's eye, Shelley saw Jackie lacing up the scarlet trainers, the fat man Lee pulling them off her then crushing her against the furthest, filthiest mattress, the one Shelley didn't lie on, the one by the wall.

"Get up." Slowly, frighteningly slowly, Shelley surfaces through tight-packed alluvial layers of grit. Her ancestors, Irish migrants who came here seeking work, changed their names and religion to blend in. Or at least that's what her mother once said; Shelley's mind is full of useless hypotheses, her lost legs tingle, difficult to locate.

"Get up off the floor." Matt bends down, takes a hold of her arm then drags her off the speckled lino and up the steep newly-carpeted stairs. It's late; no lights are on. Everything is shadowy. Her husband smells of beer and lilac and oil. While he grips her arm, Shelley once again remembers their wedding, how she crushed his fingers together while they posed for photographs. Later, in the middle of the night, he got her back.

"I love you," she whispers.

"You drunk bitch," Matt laughs and hurls her onto the king-size bed. Then he tucks in the covers, slips off his jeans and climbs in the other side.

When he broke her arm she felt it was a cleansing, a wound that took away what hope was left. She hates pain, the sheer weakness of her tendons and muscles. A long, slow death might be too much.

Matt curls up close, slides his muscular arm across her torso. It's been a year since Jackie's killer was named, and every night since then the ghost of Uncle Jed has visited, knocking loudly, while Matt sleeps, to come in. Perhaps this will be the night she makes a run for it, escapes the dot that marks her on his map. Once free, she will cry, a weird sound erupting from her diaphragm. Then she will make for the bridge, but not to jump this time, or to be rescued. Instead she will thumb a ride onto the motorway, follow signs that read "To the North."

"Open your legs." Matt parts them roughly. Shelley does not feel aroused. At first she flops as if she were unconscious then all of a sudden pushes Matt off, wrestles him down to the floor and grabs the lamp flex, wraps it tight around his pulsing neck. Next she grabs her coat, stuffs her feet into aerobics shoes, leaps out of the bedroom and vaults down the steep carpeted stairs. This is me, she thinks. This is me, living, has almost reached the doorknob when he grabs her.

"Where are you going?" Matt's neck is bleeding.

"Out." Matt takes her hand and bends it back at the wrist. Fatally, Shelley smiles, pretends to give in then just as he drops her hand makes for the door again, almost wrenching it open before he reacts.

All Good Gifts

You've come too late. This is what Donny thinks as he cradles the baby, alert and silent in its brand new clothes. He brushes the palm of his hand over its wiry scalp, breathes in the scent of some oil its mother must have rubbed it with. *Such a very long and confusing journey. And now you're here in Cumbria, poor sod.*

Reflected in its eyes he sees the bright east window. The little church is sumptuously decorated, late yellow roses wound round each pillar, leeks, marrows and dahlias piled by the font, and all this because it's Harvest Festival, when families come down from the hills and settle into their pews as they have for centuries. Mad cow: the barricades have now been lifted, and everyone is free to come and go, but there are still families he hasn't seen. It must have been this way a hundred years ago. Funny how a few months of isolation can turn a whole century on its side. But this is church, not some stupid support group. Nothing will be said about the troubles, and by the service's end fifteen boxes of food will be ready to distribute, as if there had never been any deaths.

Stephen, his son, is sitting in the pew beside him. Three days ago when Stephen drove up the farm track in a blue SUV, Donny truly thought he was seeing things.

What about its mother? Wasn't she here too? Stephen looked away. There was some big problem with the visa. In the meantime he and the kid were settling in London, where Stephen has been offered a consultancy.

London? Donny is about to sell the farm, has just been through the second worst year of his life. Couldn't Stephen stay a while?

After a supper of beans on toast, Stephen put the baby to bed, returned to the kitchen. "So, how have you been? I know these past few months have been really hard."

Hark unto the bedside manner. "Couldn't you have fucking written?"

"I was in a war zone."

"Oh, I see. *You* were in a war zone."

Elaine was standing between them, that much was clear. But there was more, a black fungus of rage settling on Donny's eyeballs. And even now, as Stephen jiggles the baby, Donny has to hold his fists in his lap.

"All good gifts around us are sent from heaven above ..."

Halfway through the service, Donny cracks. He has spent the last year perfecting the art of not crying: walking to the edges of fields when he feels his throat catch, digging his nails deep into his palms. Yet this phrase hits him without warning. As voices rise, he passes his collection money to Stephen, slips down the nave and heads for the iron-hinged door.

The church is small, built out of bluish slate and if he turns his back it disappears. Once this is done, he decides to pretend it's another weekday, eleven o'clock and time for his morning walk. Now that he has no livestock he likes to go as far as possible, to go and go until he feels lost. It's a pointless game, but the only entertainment he's discovered that satisfies his need to remain alert. Summer was hard but now that it is autumn the light and air are clear enough to revel in, the breeze sweet with just a morbid hint of the summer's wood smoke which could settle in his lungs and metastasize there, if he let it, morph into minuscule particles of the dead.

Before the crisis the footpaths were thick with ramblers, city dwellers and foreigners, dressed like explorers. Not any more. So when he hears laughter, female in pitch and somewhat foreign in tone, his adrenalin rises. It's been so long since he met anyone here he feels like some ridiculous, ancient herdsman afraid of people, tucks himself into an old sheep pen, hunkering down between ossified dung and picked-clean lamb bones, crosses his fingers and attempts to disappear.

Two women appear from behind some trees. One is a tall blonde, the other shorter, curly-haired, she's the one talking. They are dressed like hikers. Any minute now, he thinks, they will catch sight of him, his scrunched-up body in their field of vision, but instead they stop and exchange looks. Then the tall one leans down to kiss the other.

Embarrassed, Donny looks down at his hands, hands that have shoved steel prongs through the chest walls of Friesians. How they could ever manipulate a computer he cannot imagine. Sometimes a man really is too old to learn, although the stress people would have it otherwise. How they smile and nod as they listen to your drivel, examine the little chits on which you've ticked boxes as if that somehow explains how bad it gets. Lately he has noticed in himself a reluctance to grasp things, a tendency to hide tools behind his back. He closes his eyes, wills himself gone. Perhaps in a minute the women will vanish. But then someone coughs. He opens his eyes. The tall one is glaring at him. No doubt she thinks he's some kind of madman. Which he may well be, but not the kind she imagines. He gets up awkwardly, brushes grass off his knees.

"How do."

She nods back.

Time was the village would be swarming, cafes and tea shops open, even some of the farmhouses. Elaine did teas for

155

a while, but then she got sick of it, all that sitting around waiting for customers. She made a few bob while Stephen was home but after he started school refused to continue.

"The village is that way." He points behind him, back down the track. "It's not signposted, like. But it's easy to follow. Just keep your eyes peeled for the stiles." He makes a move to walk past, up to the scree, but the girls do not budge. Distantly, he makes out church bells.

"We're here to visit a friend. He's staying with his father."

Donny's stomach drops. Although it makes no sense, he knows what's coming.

"This is the name of the farm."

The note, scrawled on the back of a blank prescription, is in Stephen's handwriting. He reads it a few times, as if he is pondering, looks this way and that.

"That's my son, that is."

"You're kidding!" The shorter one laughs. The irises of her eyes are evenly divided, circles within circles, brown and blue. "Talk about synchronicity."

"What?"

She glances at her friend for a moment. They both smile.

"It's so good to meet you, Donald. I'm Ellen."

The tall blonde steps forward. "And I'm Susan."

"Susan used to work with Steve, in Sheffield. The two of them go way back."

"Oh, right." He didn't even know Stephen worked in Sheffield. What else does he not know?

"So," says Ellen, "how long have you been a farmer?"

He looks around at the moor for inspiration, remembers being ten, eleven, fourteen – at that time he had a notion to travel. Five years later he made it as far as Dover, missed the ferry and found himself turning back. He'd run out of money and anyway felt homesick, couldn't tolerate how people talked. He recalls the lamplight spilling out of the kitchen. His mother opening the door and saying nothing, just placing a piece of Bakewell tart in front of him. Since that evening he has never left.

"Oh, I don't know, since the Bronze Age."

"Really?" The blonde looks perplexed. "Well, anyways, can we offer you a ride?"

They have parked down the other side of the ridge, where the day trippers stop off for their picnics. Unable to formulate an excuse, he follows at a distance, is shown into the front seat of their estate car. Ellen gets in beside him, Susan behind.

The vehicle is brand new. Their voices sound American. He does not ask any awkward questions, mostly just listens. He hopes this is something he's learned – to be more attentive – and that in time his son will notice. It's important to Donny that Stephen remark on such changes. He wants it to be clear that he has mellowed. Otherwise his son might not return. So as they drive he focuses on Ellen, the way she interrupts when Susan is speaking. That's the way Donny was with Elaine. He also notices how Susan fidgets; her restless, fiddling fingers rolling up lint balls. They laugh and chat, and by the time they pull up outside the farm he's memorized their CD collection – REM, Jeff Buckley, Melissa Etheridge – but still does not know exactly who they are to him, or why exactly he is letting them through his gate.

Donny leaps up, but Stephen is already there to meet them, the newborn swaddled tightly against his body in some fancy foreign-looking device.

"Hi, guys!"

Stephen rushes to embrace Ellen and Susan. Amidst the kisses Donny disappears. In his day, a child was pushed about in a pram. Elaine would set the boy outside and he would chuck its chin as he passed by from milking. Looking up he can almost see young Stephen, staring down from the upstairs bedroom window, drawing silly faces on the glass. When the picture fades, Donny allows himself to notice the infant car seat, brand new and ready to go, that the women are brandishing, or is that expertly installing, on the estate car's near side. Before any thoughts have a chance to sink in he goes inside and puts on the singing kettle, tosses a few teabags into the pot. He sits and drinks thirstily at the kitchen table. But by the time the young ones have come in the tea has gone cold.

Donny lights up a smoke. Stephen winces.

"Listen, Dad, I know this must all be confusing."

Donny nods, exhales a couple of smoke rings. Stephen used to stick his hand right through them. Back then these white walls were yellow with nicotine. Even Elaine smoked one or two a day.

"Binyam's an orphan."

"Is that so?" Donny's little finger won't stop shaking.

"I guess I just wanted you to meet him."

"I thought he was yours, like."

"It all happened so fast. I had a chance to save him …"

Susan interrupts. "This must be a shock." Suddenly she, Ellen and Stephen are up on their feet again.

"I meant to explain but there was so much to do …"

"We were just planning on popping in, you know …"

Donny senses love as well as tension, feels oddly proud of his estranged son. He hadn't realized how lonely he was getting, alone up here without even a dog for company. Now the house is full. How can he get them to stay?

Ellen stares. "We thought he had told you."

"I told you I needed time." Stephen is gripping the baby by its shirt. "We haven't exactly been in close contact."

"Should we go?" Susan sounds tearful.

"No!" exclaims Ellen, standing up. Suddenly she seems wild, unable to wait, and Susan, in turn, unable to stop her.

"Hey, hey, careful!" Donny pushes forward. "Give me the bairn." Ellen steps back. The transfer is made and soon the child is sucking on a seam in his jacket.

"This is what you used to do."

His son shrugs. "I can't believe I was ever quite that helpless."

Donny sits down. The infant must be teething, its spit hot and foamy all over his neck. What do they do with the dead where he comes from? Running his finger over the boy's ear-lobe Donny gets an inkling of how big the world is. Of how isolated he's been, here in this village, lost in the tedious details of one epidemic. He reaches out a hand. Stephen flinches.

"This is going to be difficult."

Ellen rolls her eyes. "Don't you think we know?"

***

"Are you there, Adele?"

When he enters, nothing is moving. The house is concrete, and the noise from the road echoes around its emptiness, the place where the girl last sat eating maize porridge, a rickety plastic chair with uneven legs. He knows she has two broth-ers, but not where they are now, this dark, cool interior barred by sunlight a home no adult has entered for over three years.

"Adele?"

She said he could visit. And so he has come, bearing juicy oranges and flip-flops: he does not want to use force. He decides to step further, into the unlocked home with its win-dow cloths flapping.

159

Adele's younger brothers ran off to the city. He tries to imagine them: begging, carrying luggage, parking people's cars if they are lucky. If not, well … A scorpion appears, brandishing cracked claws.

"Adele?"

Behind the scorpion, a patterned blanket; laid on the blanket an infant, panting thirstily. He kneels down, reaches out a finger and strokes it gently across the infant's palm.

***

Martha Onuyayo is not a suspicious woman. Yet as she shakes Susan's hand, Stephen notices a certain reserve.

"Binyam is very fortunate. May God protect you both, and your new family."

"Th-thank you," stutters Susan, equally unlike herself.

"The paperwork is all complete."

Stephen places his hand on Susan's shoulder. He remembers, for a second, what she looked like, that night back in Sheffield: a young, brilliant intern with short hair and flashing earrings, leaning over a table to pass him her wallet. Inside: pictures of home, tall trees, wide rivers; a man and a woman up to their waists in grass.

Since she arrived they have kissed only once: a strange, drunken moment better forgotten, despite the fact that they are now legally married. Does she still drink Pernod? Why is he doing this? Martha Onuyayo was married for five years. Then her husband died. Luckily for her, his brother did not force her to remarry but helps her out financially, Martha's five offspring raised alongside these poor orphans. Such boundless kindness. His own motives altogether murkier.

"We value your husband highly," grins Martha, relaxing, "his work assists us greatly. We are sad to lose him."

"Yes," replies Susan, "I am sure. He's a wonderful doctor."

"I will come for Binyam next week, when his passport is issued. He will travel back to the UK with me." Stephen grips Susan's shoulder, feels her push back. Later she will accuse him of lying, of neglecting to inform her about this, and when she does he'll explode as if he has become his father. But right now he is calm.

"I hear you have a position already, in London."

"Yes. Yes, I do." He will miss Martha. He will miss Kenya. He will also miss Adele. The last time he saw her, she was en route to Nairobi. A skinny thirteen-year-old with sores on her arms, she thanked him politely for taking care of her child before handing back the drugs that he had given her.

"I do not need these, Sir. But you do."

"Susan," asks Martha, "do you also work as a doctor?"

"Please, Stephen," whispers Susan. "It's time to go."

***

"Does it run in the blood?"

"What?" Donny cracks a lager. He hasn't dared drink since the crisis started. But tonight when Stephen came home with a six-pack he decided he would do what it took to get close.

"Cowardice."

"Eh? I don't know what you mean."

"I suppose not." Stephen takes a swig. "So tell me, Dad, did they all just die?"

"I killed them myself. All seventy five."

"Christ."

After Elaine did not return, Julie Burnham filled up Donny's fridge with casseroles. She said that as a neighbour she felt responsible, and for a while Donny wore his better shoes. But nothing happened, and when the fridge emptied she did not refill it. Ten years later it was Donny who came visiting, this time in a government-issue gas mask. He shot all her ewes then one week later returned again, this time to throw their corpses onto a pyre. Julie even tried to thank him, gave him a rich Dundee cake for his troubles. He turned it down.

"Did you know it's blokes like you that put the knife in, educated bastards from the city who think they know everything but don't know fuck-all?"

"And did you know it's blokes like you who think AIDS can be cured?"

"What do you mean? I thought it could."

"Well, guess what, Dad, sometimes bugs get resistant."

Father and son, still taking the mick. Donny cracks open another lager. He doesn't really know what else to say. Elaine's bits and pieces are ash now, mostly, and the one remaining painting up for sale. He's made more progress in these few days than in all the eighteen years since his marriage combusted. But something still hangs over him.

"Did you ever hit Mum?"

What the hell is this about? "No I didn't, sonny. No, I never did."

"That's not what I remember."

Donny stands up. "What is it you want from me, Stephen?"

"I don't know, Dad."

"Because you know I don't have a lot."

"I'm going to bed now."

But he doesn't. Instead he pulls on his boots and heads outside, leaves the door banging, uneven gunshots, and that night Donny dreams he is late for work. When he walks into the toilets he has his hands in his pockets, is fumbling with a handful of small change. He has just smoked a fag. He is looking down at the floor, at the muddy footprints that are already messing up the tiles and thinking about his mop, the way it exudes filth no matter how many times he wrings it when the first blow comes to the back of his head. Oh Jesus, he thinks, this is it. Some nutcase is killing him over the weekend. The junkies who hate him because he's always around, mopping and rinsing and collecting 10p pieces, so they can't deal or shoot up in peace. His chin hits the floor, several teeth break off and when he wakes up the farmhouse is empty. He knows this because his veil has suddenly lifted, horizontal light alive through each room.

Bring him back. Bring back my son.

The child's little travel cot is empty.

If Stephen's done a runner he'll bloody kill him.

Donny grabs his keys and jumps onto his bike, freewheels quickly down towards the road. Stephen's car is there, which is a good sign. But Donny still feels weird. He abandons the bike, struggles through the copse up to the railway station. Perhaps, with the sale of the farm, he can set up a business, go back to casual labour, apprentice in something. *Elaine*, whisper his fingers. *Elaine, Elaine.* Yes, at the very least he has his body, strong despite the years, not yet destroyed.

He finds them up in the lookout, behind the sycamores, creeps quietly up the ridge above the tracks. The bloodied dots in the necks of headless chickens; the limp brush of a fox, brandished aloft: so much about life round here is furtive, the taking of liberties in order to free someone else.

"How do."

"Dad!" Stephen jumps. His face looks soft, blurry, like a dish of cold custard.

"What are you doing out here? I thought you were sleeping."

The child is swaddled tight against Stephen's body. Donny wonders how it can possibly breathe.

"I had this idea."

"You did, did you?"

"But I think it's no good," sighs Stephen. "There's no point pretending."

Donny extends his hands and then withdraws them. Is his son perhaps sick? Don't go, he thinks, don't leave me here. "Can I at least make you some egg and bacon?"

"That would be grand. And maybe some milk for the boy."

Back home, Donny cracks six, tips them into one of Elaine's old basins. Whipping them hard he thinks he is fine, but as the burner ignites, begins to retch: fifty ewes, bloated with decomposition, their eyeballs rapidly turning to maggoty mush: like Beelzebub or some other deathless demon he will always be lighting them on fire, watching their bodies melt to reveal what they carried.

At least Binyam made it out alive.

***

"You do not have to leave."

"Yeah, right."

Doctor Khan leans forward. "Listen, young man. You are in the right place. We can treat you here. There is no problem."

"I made a mistake."

"You made a mistake. That does not mean your patients, the children, need suffer."

"They already have."

"What do you mean?"

"My mind isn't on the job. Isn't that obvious?"

"Take a break. Go home. But come back! We need you. I'll write you a prescription. You can fill it anywhere. You know the drill as well as I."

Outside the compound, Stephen dons his dark glasses. There's someone he should see, maybe tomorrow. That girl he met in the hotel, on the staircase: a legitimate addition to his caseload and the only local who knows the awkward truth. Adele: her shy smile, the sadness with which she moved, conserving energy. Just like Maria, he thinks, now; the woman he visited, intending just to talk but unable to stop himself. He only visited her twice, but twice was enough.

***

At six they all sit down, eat leftover pasta, and after dinner the young ones go to the pub. They seem to have made it up, at least for the moment, and while they are gone, Donny starts a fire. Not inside the house, but out in the meadow. It's time he finally tackled the stuff in the shed.

The sky is turning green around its edges. He stands too close, welcomes the scorching heat. The dresses are perfect relics from the eighties. As he drops each garment into the fire it flares up for a second. Watching the sparks rise up and scatter, Donny feels better than he has for weeks. For some strange reason his rage has shrunk down to nothing, leaving a space so blue and softly luxurious he wonders what its name is, what he should call it. Stephen will be fine, he rationalizes. He has a job, friends, a strong moral compass. As for the baby, Donny feels relieved. His heart contracted painfully when he held it, contracts again now, thinking of its mother, but a man can't raise a bairn alone.

He will wait until they leave. Then he will do it. He'd like to stay but it's all gone, his bloody-mindedness, his sense of tradition, his connection to the tough old sods who came before. An owl hoots, off in the trees, a burnt twig crackles.

He knew she was gone in the moment before waking. Coming downstairs he remembers seeing Stephen, slumped in front of the morning television. "She's gone, hasn't she?"

"Yep."

That was it for shared grieving. At the funeral, neither of them spoke. Once, before Stephen left home, Donny tried a letter, but the words came out wrong. He ripped it into confetti.

A bruise is a bruise.

When the fire is done, he douses it with water. Then a pair of eyes pierces the darkness: Elaine loved the night. She would go for long walks. At first he resisted, but then after a while he let her go.

Underneath the World

"WATCH OUT, NUTMEG, THERE'S A CAR COMING."

"The dragon's hungry it eated you you are deaded but watch this Mommy I am brave I come to rescue you I have a water pistol it shoots out fire peeyow peeyow yay I killed the dragon I killed the dragon but it's hungry I think it's waking up uh-oh Mommy Mommy feed it some dead baddies quick before it eats us QUICK QUICK!"

Thursday, 3:15 p.m.: Cynthia and Fee cross the road, Cynthia thinking about Happy Hour, not so much the ritual but the concept. She never drank before Fee was born, but now she has a glass or two every evening. Fee calls it Mummy Juice, which Cynthia doesn't mind, although the other day at preschool Fee, who is almost four, enquired during Circle Time why it was that kids could not drink booze. Her head in the art cupboard, this being Volunteer Tuesday, Cynthia quietly died and came back to life, all the while peeling gossamer glue-skin off scissor blades.

Later that same day, Fee also reported to a newly-wed neighbour that in her mom's opinion marriage is "shavery." "But I don't think so. Do you? I'm going to marry Neon." Neon lives on the other side and is in grade three. She also has a trampoline and a unicycle.

Five years ago, Cynthia thought small children oblivious, their memories like voice mail, erased every morning, but now it feels like life under the Stasi, her every treacherous act recorded verbatim, scrambled a little, perhaps, but still on tape.

"Here is your rope. Pull on it, Mommy! Pull on it!"

When Daniel first left, Cynthia felt as if she had been cancelled, her long name reduced to a sinister X. Not X as in treasure or x's and o's, but the sign of the plague, a mark designed to inspire horror. This is my X, she imagined him saying to his girlfriends, his naked back heroically hunched like Jesus's, the cross that I forever have to bear.

Since Dan moved out he has lost several pounds, the result of couch surfing and living on pizza. But he says he's okay, good, in fact, the determined jut of his jaw a testament to friendship, in particular to that of François Belmont, Daniel's best bud from The Pas. François owns a chain of high-end art stores and has installed Dan as store manager in one of them. Wouldn't you know it, thinks Cynthia, pulling on her rope, Dan the old hockey nerd suddenly knee-deep in acrylics. And what's more, Frank is currently married to Layne, the bleached-blonde, French-Canadian alt-country artiste. From barista to Graceland in one fell swoop. How the hell did Daniel manage it? Meanwhile Cyn crawls about, picking up mangled raisins and miniature hard hats, bumping her head on the half-stripped kitchen table where her fortune still waits in the form of a business plan for Devilish Diapers!, red and black napkins with little forked tails she thought she might get launched in time for Halloween. That, and writing year-end reports for a firm of undertakers.

"Hey Mom, Dude wants a hot chocolate."

Dude is a rat, floppy and horribly lifelike.

"No, chicken, we are not getting any hot chocolate."

"Oh!" Fee pouts. "Now Dude is really mad."

One day Cynthia will call these the Playmobil years, dozens of the little plastic figures arranged across her desk in ironic tableaux. Some days, she still attempts to work amongst them, curled up on her side, laptop ajar. Yet two little chunks of two hours a week – the times her daughter Fiona is in preschool – are just not enough in which to jump-start her career, so instead Cynthia guzzles tea and eats chocolate, moves the little brainless dolls around.

"Look! Here we are!" Cyn does her best to sound excited. The truth is she's dreading what's to come. She has only agreed to go because Jude bribed her: if she meets someone at the party and brings home their number Jude will bake her up a batch of brownies. Meanwhile Fee is out of her mind with joy.

Jude lives in an adorable heritage cottage, all on one floor with a yard out back and out front. Jude is a single mother also, with two small boys she conceived via the same sperm donor. As soon as Fee arrives, Rocky and Albert strip off their clothes and drag her off to the sand box to play dragons. That leaves Cyn free to chat with Jude, an experience she values arguably more highly than a Jesuit might an audience with the Pope.

"Darling! You look delicious. That pumpkin colour really suits you. Come on in. We're making wine from grass."

The kitchen is filled with pans and plastic tubs most of which have dead grass and water in them, as well as finger paint and what looks like sick.

"Don't worry, Cyn, it's only flour. I was trying to make play dough you know but forgot the recipe. Maybe I should add some chocolate chips."

Jude is six foot two and thin as a supermodel even though she left ballet years ago. Somehow she has also managed to raise her two ruffians without resorting to murder, or even daycare; Cyn still doesn't quite understand how, attempted once to take this personally, as an insult, then just gave up because Jude is so much fun. Not that Jude doesn't have her off days: Cyn has seen her, clad in slippers, running down the alley after Bert, who rarely falls asleep before midnight. She knows the three of them eat at the Burger King regularly, is also aware that Jude occasionally disappears, off to the bars or perhaps the beach, leaving the boys with some confused house guest or other, only to return three days later with a big, fat smile and brand new Bionicles. Once, she knows for a fact, the boys were left alone for over three hours when their uncle had to leave to catch a plane. According to Fee they ate frozen cookie dough, gave each other baths filled with washing-up liquid and were more or less okay, but Cyn still worries. It gives her something to feel self-righteous about.

"And how's our Elvis?"

Jude has called Dan this ever since she heard about Layne, whom she is convinced has designs. In Jude's mind, Dan is angling too, and has moved in with François as a strategy. Dan is also clearly a frustrated artist, this being Jude's analysis of pretty much everybody.

"Oh fine, fine. He takes Fee for ice cream, drives her over to the Bay and buys her T-shirts then disappears for a week. He's changed so much it's positively creepy, walks like a businessman and even wears slip-ons, claims to covet a mansion in West Vancouver. I think it was all in his genes, on timed release."

"What do you mean – he hit thirty and it suddenly struck him, like reverse schizophrenia or something?"

"Yes, triggered by stress, the stress of inaction. Too much lying on the couch reading Deepak Chopra."

"You thought he was a slacker but he wasn't."

"Exactly. I guess I'm just not happening enough for him, financially, professionally, whatever. Pretty ironic, given that he's unemployed. Was unemployed."

"And now you are."

"What do you mean? I'm a stay-at-home mom, a resting diplomat, an under-the-table mompreneur. God, Jude, do you have any drugs or alcohol? I'm frigging desperate."

"I thought you were on the wagon, AA and all that."

"Ha! With you as my sponsor? I'm about as likely to be sworn in as Finance Minister."

"Ah well, maybe a few drops of Mummy Juice … Oh my God, what's that?" Something flies past them, out of the playroom.

"Dude's head."

"Okay, who decapitated the rat?" Jude yells but no one answers. Peering round the door, Cyn observes a huddle of naked, face painted children squeezed in between the play kitchen and the couch.

"Pretend I had a penis and a vagina," whispers Fee.

"Yeah, me too." She and Rocky conspiratorially giggle.

Cyn elbows Jude. "Let's crack open the vino, Fatso. Come on."

Skinflint and Fatso are their names for each other. Skinflint for Cyn, who is always broke, Fatso for Jude, whose lack of body fat can be positively alarming, at least to those who have never seen her eat. Together they sit at the pock-marked kitchen table and devour leftover pizza, a container of Timbits and several handfuls of pre-washed wilted spring greens while Cyn gulps and Jude sips at the Cab-Sauve.

"Not bad."

"No, not bad at all."

The crows are migrating again past the window, flecks of black against an orange sky. Every evening they commute from downtown streets to distant roosts in the suburbs. Fee insists on calling them blackbirds, is convinced they go to bed each night on the moon.

171

"So why do you think they call this Happy Hour?"

Jude shrugs, nonplussed.

"Because it's the moment most of us want to die."

"Have you ever tried it?"

"What? Crying Woolf, so to speak?"

"Yes, actually."

"No, actually. Although I did once stick my head in a gas oven. I was trying to clean it but accidentally turned it on. Mary, my old roommate found me. I was out of it, you know, but not quite unconscious. I'd do it again. Not to die or anything. It just felt … edgy. Mary was incredibly jealous because she didn't get there first. Attempts were all the rage in those days."

"I remember that. Once when I was sixteen I made a noose. I strung it from a hook in my bedroom ceiling but it pulled down half the plaster, couldn't hold the weight. And that was before I put my neck inside it."

"Well, good job. Otherwise I'd have no babysitter."

"Speaking of which, are you sure this is still okay?"

"Yes, yes, of course. Look at them. They're Edenic, already regressed back to the Bronze Age. Soon they'll be erecting a Lego Stonehenge."

Indeed, the kids are engrossed, mixing up mud-coloured tempera from massive bottles and dipping wads of ripped-up diaper into it. Jude rolls a cigarette. If there is a more laid-back way of parenting, Cyn can't imagine it being legal. She tiptoes softly into the play room and kisses Fiona on the cheekbone, breathes in her scent of yeast, fresh air.

"When you come home, Mommy, I will be a dino-saur."

"And why is that, chicken?"

"Because I am a lump of slime right now."

Jude waves her off theatrically, blows kisses. Meanwhile Cyn walks tall, desperate to appear Amazonian on this, her first night in search of a date.

The singles party ends up giving her lockjaw. Groups of ugly, mad-looking men and women herded from table to table by overdressed hostesses, forced to describe themselves in three-minute sound bites before a buzzer goes and everyone cheers. Although she has prepared a witty spiel, when her turn comes Cyn just can't stop smiling, and it's not how it looks. Luckily her neighbour, a short, fat brunette with thinning hair done up in faux-tortoiseshell barrettes, takes the cue and steps excitedly forward, allowing Cyn time to step outside the ballroom and do her best to pop her jaw back in. "Fuck," she whispers, reopening her jaw experimentally only to hear it crack like a melting iceberg. Suddenly a man is in her way.

"Does that hurt?"

"No, not really."

The man is short, about five two, with thick eyeglasses and a strange green suit on. Under the fluorescent lights of the hotel lobby its texture resembles that of wholegrain bread. Cyn wonders if it's hemp, or perhaps buckwheat. Possessed by an urge to touch it, she braids her fingers.

"I'm Keith: travel bags and real estate."

"Cynthia: novelty diapers and Playmobil."

"Wow, my little guys love that stuff. Have you seen the gladiators?"

"I do the girly things, you know, fairies, princesses, exact replicas of household cleaning products."

"Fancy swapping cards?"

"Sure, why not."

Keith Mann, The Travel Bag Emporium.

"Thanks. Great." Cynthia Quest, The Plywood Desk in the Living Room Littered with Detritus. "Actually, whoops, I ran out of business cards, sorry."

Ten minutes later they are having a drink. Keith is odd, but at least he likes her, which is more than she could say for Dan. So although she feels uncomfortable, Cyn decides to be generous. The highballs are great, and after all what's a wee chat.

"My ex is now a Country and Western singer. Well, trying to be. And I'm a small businesswoman but I don't like to say that, in case anyone steals my ideas."

"My wife just left."

Cyn starts making a swan out of her napkin, and by the time she looks up, Keith is on the verge of crying, tears swelling up along the pink rims of his eyes.

Fee's forehead is dewy with sweat, her limbs flung sideways as if in motion. Cyn pulls the covers back up over her, taking care not to disturb Dude. The rat's neck is bleeding foam, flecks of it, dry gore, across the cartoon comforter. Cyn picks them off, stuffs them back in. Across the room, in Rocky's toddler bed, Albert and Rocky are entwined in sleep, eight-year-old Bert with his head on his younger brother's chest.

It's just after twelve by the kitchen clock. Cyn finds herself remembering the rigid C-shape she slept in, baby beside her, when Fee was new and she and Dan exhausted. Often she would wake mere seconds before Fee did, as if allowed two breaths before the cry.

It wasn't all lovely. Once, when Fee had a terrible cold, she nursed over twenty times in just eight hours, and Cyn fantasized double self mastectomy. Cut the things off, she implored herself, just let the kid have them, milky, bloody cushions to cling to and suckle on. But then she felt guilty, afraid she was tempting fate.

So much about motherhood is superstitious. Still is – the ritual sniff Cyn gives to Fee's little pajamas on mornings Fee is at preschool or a sitter's, the required, daily "I love you" to ward off disaster, especially if there has been a tantrum or fight. As she leaves the kids' room, Jude touches the letters on one of its name plates: B, E, R, T spells Bert.

"So where is your man?"

Jude glides into the kitchen, mysterious with moonlight, hair wild and unraveled down her back, and for a moment Cyn wonders if it was Jude speaking, or just some guilt-producing voice in her head.

"What?"

"The man you met tonight – don't tell me you didn't."

Cyn laughs. "Yeah, right: sixteen point two for originality, minus eight for talent and good looks."

"Dear oh dear. Ah, well, I sense the presence of excellent anecdote material."

"No, Jude. It was just bad. Anyway, I'm not really ready."

There's a pause.

"Are they all asleep?"

"Yes, ma'am."

"Well, grab the scotch and come into my bedroom. Yours is freezing. One of the windows is cracked."

"Now she tells me."

Cyn experiences a flutter of anticipation. She doesn't know what to think, prefers not to, fumbles inside the top cupboard for the Glenmorangie. Two chinking glasses, a tin-foil ashtray: smoking in bed is very, very bad indeed. She kicks off her shoes and climbs into the vast, creamy acreage of Jude's old king size, pours out a generous couple of fingers each, listens to Jude lighting up her last prize joint.

"I killed the plants, you know. They were just too prolific."

"Mm-hm."

"Could you open the window?"

Cyn observes the edges of her consciousness loosening, as if a wind were billowing up, stretching its fabric. The word "firmament" rotates in her mind's eye, first upwards and then downwards. Her glass is put down and her clothes taken off, skin against skin like something uncooked, the sensation of warmth across her pelvis suddenly grown excruciatingly specific.

First one and then the other; Jude's breasts with their dark areolas attached to a familiar, slender ribcage that Cyn finds she can circle with outstretched hands. When she finally falls asleep the Gorgon face of Cyn's conscience has a smile on it also, the jangled nerves of its locks smoothed out and tame now, motion that's been transformed into light.

"Need to go poo-poo." Two little eyes stare out at her through the pre-dawn mirk; Cyn rolls over, registers a headache.

"Mama's asleep, Rocky, let me help you." The clock's rectangular face glows with red stitches, 5:03 a.m. Rocky grabs her hand, pulls Cyn over to the bathroom where she tugs down his big-boy diaper and cleans up the mess. Rocky will not go back to bed, so she wraps them both in a blanket and sits on the couch.

"And on *Saturday* he ate one slice of salami, one piece of cake …"

Cyn leans back, rests her chin on Rocky's head. A huge Indian bedspread hangs from the ceiling, billows over the two of them like a cloud. The bedspread is patterned with green and red swirls.

Once, shortly after Dan left, Fee and Cyn lay curled beneath a heavy blanket. "Look, Mama," said Fee, "we are underneath the world." Cyn remembers how comforted yet afraid she was, as if the earth above might just crash down. Everyone needs a refuge, but what is the difference between feeling safe and being buried alive? Cyn starts to suffocate. Suddenly the hungry caterpillar has become a butterfly, Rocky's body is limp, and Jude is before her, resplendent in an orange satin kimono.

"Your son and my daughter are sleeping together. I just thought you should know."

Jude slides onto the couch, rolls Rocky against her.

"Should I go make coffee?" Cyn suddenly feels rather cold.

"Sure." Jude looks distant, distracted. Dan used to call her Artemis, The Unattainable, a reference to Jude's wide circle of jilted admirers. As Cyn tips the beans into the grinder she registers a surprising degree of wistfulness. *If only* last night were a typical night.

Fee races into the kitchen, her mottled bum and bare feet jiggling with joy. "Mommy, Bert and I are on our honeymoon!"

Cyn scoops her up, whirls her round and narrowly avoids the kettle. "I thought you were marrying Neon?"

"We're all getting married. Me, Bert and Neon, all together. There's going to be a party this afternoon."

"Well I don't want to." Bert frowns, his mouth pursed. Tall and thin, he spans the bedroom doorway, all scooped-out angles and surprising asymmetry.

"But *I* do!" Fee wriggles down and pushes Bert, who staggers backwards, recovers and pushes her back. Fee then falls into a basket of dirty laundry. Watching her rise with a towel on her head Cyn can't tell if Fee's trembling is anger or laughter. As Fee's wail rises in pitch, Cyn opts to distract.

"Come on. Let's make eggy toast. Let's make it together."

Rocky runs in, Cyn opens the fridge, gets the kids messily cracking eggs, and soon they are all sitting down to stale hunks of rye bread, lacy with well-cooked omelette and glistening with syrup, and when Jude, now dressed, plants a dry, passionless kiss on one side of her forehead Cyn finds she does not mind as much as she thought she might. One day soon she will finally emerge from her bolt-hole, transform from plastic idea into living person. Meanwhile, she must rethink her family tableau. First of all, remove Barista Daddy: hurl him in deep behind the television. Second, move Astronaut Mommy further forward. She can always give them new heads, later on.

Lion of the Heart

DRIVING HERE, THE FOREST DISSOLVED. Shay's fear
was at the wheel, a fish hook cast in shallows, sinking
through darkness, seeking something soft to enter and hold.
Now that she has slept, the place feels even eerier. A pair of
wool socks, rank with sweat, draped over the back of an old
cane rocking chair; old boots, relics from the seventies. What
belonged to whom? Shay craves a drink. Instead she sits at the
desk, breathes in and out and notices the flurry in a feather.
An eagle feather, pinned up like a sign.

Something terrible happened out here; nothing anyone
living can remember. *Claw marks on the sill. A dark shape
blurring behind spring leaves:* the memory gone, undone by
shock, the pressure inside a skull of blood and fluid. *Ron and
I walking up the ridge: Ron is wearing a red and white
bandanna, both of us are singing* Let It Be.

Shay stands in a dark room filled with paper. The room is
not hers. It belonged to her mother, a woman whose face
was frequently hidden by hair. Lovely hair: a deep reddish-
brown; hair that was never dyed, unlike her daughter's,
which is blonde and turning black again at the roots. *I take
pain pills three times a day and avoid coffee because it gives
me heartburn, live in a cabin up on a ridge with a view of the
jagged terrain where the animal found us. I do not expect to
marry, know I that will likely never feel joy. But there are
days when the ocean shines, and across it freighters and tug-
boats slide as if there were no such thing as dumb bad luck.*

179

A list of countries follows: Brazil, Honduras, Grenada, Northern Ireland, Iran, Iraq. A sketch of a face with no eyes, just a mouth and nose then some line from a poem, enclosed in quotation marks: *Roar, lion of the heart, and tear me open!*

Ron said all that mattered was the present. I was intoxicated. I thought he was brilliant. All that stuff about risk, about welcoming snakes. But now we are apart, in different realms. Everything divides, and not all divisions are random: death, life, love; hate; one season, the next.

As the sun comes up Shay stands on the deck. She knows the place where it happened is close by. She has seen the map. It is pinned on a wall, ragged and torn, with a hole where Caroline's finger rested too often, on the grey speckled ridge between two burgeoning creeks.

Ron Stein was twenty-three; almost the age Shay is now. The single photo of him confirms every stereotype: blond, bearded hiker in flares and blue headband, eyes hidden behind big shades, arm around the trunk of some old, massive cedar: a man with no doubt about his oncoming future. Her mother refused to talk about her ex. Yet here in this cabin Ron is a saint, a saint who was never buried and whose dreams glow, numinous. And somewhere out there his vertebrae lie scattered.

In England our biggest animals were roe deer, the odd wild pony – nothing to fear, nothing to get too worked up about. Pretty boring, really! Last night on the couch, Shay pushed her off, rolled into a defensive, fetal ball. She did not want it then and does not now: Caroline's clipped voice with its pretended coolness. Caroline in her post-Ron days, as journalist, who followed impossible conflicts, reduced them to fact-filled arguments.

Shay switches on a lamp. Half a dried beetle falls from its shade while a moth sits, quietly crucifying, on the outlet, waiting to be zapped by escaping sparks. The cabin has four rooms and a tiny back deck, sits on the side of a mountain, five miles from a road. A place that fills in the ellipses of her childhood, for this is where Caroline went when things got difficult. This is where she escaped when she couldn't cope. Yet Shay might never have known it even existed were it not for Gillian, who let slip the name of the place one evening in Masset. It was the last evening of her fieldwork contract, and for once Shay's boss relaxed. Gill knew Jack and Caroline back in the eighties, could not believe that Shay has never been here.

Caroline's chair is warm from the fire. This must be where she sat, writing. A photograph of her rests against a mug. She is young and beautiful, freckle-faced, dressed in a collarless shirt of blue striped cheesecloth.

Was she afraid? It's hard to tell from the picture, which is bright and blurry in that sentimental way Shay's never noticed about what few snapshots exist of her. *You think you suffered? You never even knew you were born:* Caroline's last words. The past tense struck Shay as odd, but she didn't think anything more of it at the time. Her mother often disappeared. Jack usually said she was visiting friends. Wrapped in a Mexican blanket she never knew existed, Shay looks around, searches for evidence.

Jack must have been here today or yesterday, surely. He drove out that day like a man on a secret mission. And she knew from the set of his jaw he'd be gone for a while. Rifling again through the books on the desk she finds a diagram sketched in what looks like his hand. *Here, here* or *here*: three points on a line. It's 4 a.m.

"Go outside." That is what he always suggested. Cursing the dark she shoves the note in her pocket, pulls on coat and boots and does as she's told.

Ron laughs. Caroline slips out of her shirtwaist. A year ago she was still in deepest Nottingham. Now look at her: lying in a beautiful room with a man who loves her, the first bloke who ever called her wise.

The next thing he said was "What is your animal totem?" He said his was bear. She just about wet her knickers. Now he is underneath her and inside her. Blue mountains, blue sky: who could imagine seeing both from their living room?

Ron smiles. His grey eyes are flecked with glass. His body oiled with sweat, a driftwood sculpture. Caroline runs her hand right down through it, comes to rest on his penis. Then she sits up, crosses her legs and pulls out the rope of her hair from between her breasts. Ron reaches for his pouch, begins rolling a joint. Caroline salivates. She loves the way his hands move, certain yet graceful, the nails on his left hand short, the others long.

"Had a dream last night."

"What about?"

"Eagle came down and called me up to the mountains, a very precise spot, up on Bobcat Ridge."

"Do you think we should go?"

"Yep. First thing tomorrow."

"I've got work."

"Well, quit."

Jack picks up the Friendly Diner's menu. It's stained with egg, which he scratches off with his finger, decides on a muffin, one of those raisin-brain ones with a top like a thatched roof.

"What can I get you?"

The waitress has a mole on her upper lip. He turns to the window, mumbles into his stubble. "Coffee and a muffin."

"Okay then. Can I take this away?"

As the waitress peels the menu out of his fingers he wonders what he must look like. Some sort of nut. The day they met he was dapper and trim: a newly-fledged Animal Science professor, in a rush to get to morning class. Caroline was waiting. Did he have time to read over her article, check it for accuracy? She was writing about timber wolves. A woman of about thirty, with clear green eyes. Her face was cut through with scars like a horror-film zombie and he didn't know where or how to look.

You would think it would block all communication, that layer of scar tissue placed between self and other, mock every comment, every thought. But it was surprising how quickly he got used to it, her misassembled jigsaw of puckered features. Over time, as they talked and dined, he began to lose his initial curiosity and understand that he was falling in love. For twenty-six years he lived with that face, with Caroline's refusal to admit defeat, even through infections and surgeries, her terrible weeks of rage and despair, colluding with her secrecy about Bear Creek, the secret address where pain still lived, a place no one else could visit or even know about.

It was his fault, of course, for not taking charge. The day Shay was born he dropped the umbilical clamp and had to watch the nurse as she snipped and swabbed, performing the ritual he had been assigned. And then when Caroline asked for help, he found he could barely tolerate the baby's fragility. So terrified was he of squashing or breaking its body that it was days before he could give her a ten-minute break.

He has told Shay he is going off camping. She's a scientist, too — and a damn good one. He supposes this means she has turned out all right, although since her mother's death she has been argumentative.

"Why wasn't she medicated? Did she ever see a doctor?"

"Ron Stein never believed in therapy. He said it was bogus. That she should trust in the power of meditation." Caroline's loyalty to Ron enraged Jack. But he never questioned it, his respect her undoing.

Is Shay better off without him? Of course not. He attacks his muffin. He will need to eat if he plans to go on.

The sun is almost up. Ron is inside. Caroline sits on the rock and watches for colours. As the light spreads, different flowers catch: a sudden star of lupin or Indian paintbrush. She can hear nothing human, not even breathing: her own chest almost still with awe. They have lived here only seven weeks. The cabin is finished. The city and its diversions suddenly invisible: from here she can only see the ocean indirectly, a buzz of blue mosquitoes beside white cloud. Today Ron wants to hike up to the ridge. They've seen a grizzly and her cubs wandering across the alpine. Ron is curious. He thinks we fear animals far too much. It's strange to her, the strength of his conviction: a kind of innocence she both mistrusts and adores. Back in the restaurant everyone rolled their eyes when he walked in and demanded breakfast at seven one evening. *Why should we live by clocks, like factory workers? Isn't it time we freed ourselves from the compulsion to produce?* It was ridiculous, and yet she wanted to protect him. Quietly, without telling the others, she fried him up two eggs and put them on toast. It was the kind of place a person could do that. Hearing the door to the cabin open and close, she endures a pang of regret. Could she not go back?

"Did you see them yet today?"

"No."

"But they're up there. Come on, let's skip breakfast. Take some blueberries and bread up in a bag."

"Don't you think it's risky, taking food? What if the mother bear smells it?"

"I *want* her to smell it. In fact, I want her to eat it. Don't you think it's time we got to meet her up close?"

Ron takes her face in his hands and she flushes a little. He smells of sweat and wood smoke, a trace of grass.

It is utterly dark. Shay stumbles over a rock and twists her ankle, curses loudly into the humming night. For Christ's sake, why did he have to go and do this: leave without any explanation? Hasn't she suffered enough?

The crosses are possible campsites. This is what she has decided. Jack will be at one, and she will take him home. But she doesn't know the land and she is frightened. As the sky lightens, she grows tired, weak. Why didn't she eat? When she finds Jack she will ream him out. Did he take any food? The secrets in their house like sleeping giants, massive, snoring bodies you had to creep around. How cramped they were, even in that big house.

"Shay? Is that you?"

His voice an alarm: she runs, unsure, asleep.

"I'm sorry. I just had to bring your mother." Jack is squatting underneath a tarpaulin, the jar of Caroline's ashes in his hands.

"Please, forgive me."

She has found him in the very last place, the place she would have left and given up from: a rocky spot backing onto the alpine, beautiful and potentially deadly.

"So is this where it happened?"

"I don't know." Jack turns to her. Shay can see his exhaustion. Instead of speaking she takes his hand and holds it to her, runs it slowly over the warmth of her face.

Jack said when he found her, she was wearing make-up.

Caroline had a skin graft that never took, her body rejecting itself, over and over, the stench of rotting flesh plus disinfectant a smell they could never quite get out of the house. Pristine rolls of bandages, wrapped in plastic; her mother sitting silent as a sculpture, a bust made of flesh that seethed with impatience, disgust.

"Let's go home," says Shay.

"First we scatter her ashes."

"Okay. Just as the sun comes up."

They sit together back to back, father and daughter sharing water and crackers, passing them back and forth as daylight arrives.

"Do you think he was a saint?"

"Who? Ron Stein?" Despite himself, Jack begins to shiver. Shay, ever the adult, rubs his back.

"No, but I don't think he was the asshole I always wanted him to be. He was just some young guy."

"Do you think she was ever happy?"

Jack doesn't answer.

For years she thought she wanted to move to London. Screw small towns, cities were where it was at. Yet now she is in paradise, and it is not a city, or a park. It is a mountain, a series of peaks, pink snow streaking between fallen boulders, frozen air entirely free of use. Ron feeds her a handful of fat, sweet blueberries and she feels the juice run cold down her throat. As the wind comes up, taking her sweat scent with it, she turns to Ron for a kiss and closes her eyes. She's bitten her lip; there is blood in her mouth.

Two days ago a black bear came, wandered around the cabin, hungry and curious. It stood up on its hind legs at the sill and for a moment she was struck dumb, unable to shoo it.

The bear left its mark, three long, blond scratches, and today even with her eyes closed she can still see it: an animal loping purposefully off through the meadow. Two others, following behind.

Ravenous Hours

"GUESS WHO'S ABOUT TO HAVE LUNCH," asks Jeffrey. "Come on, close your eyes. I'll lead you over there."

Seen from the side, Gloria is a freak of nature. Earlier this week she got stuck between cars and had to be oiled and released by leering security guards. "About to pop?" asked the fat one. "No," whispered Gloria, wincing, "I've three months left to go."

She could have said something rude, but decided not to. It's not as if she could easily run away. With a bump that already threatens to tip her over, she is slow moving, and even with her eyes closed senses the stares. *Pregnant with twins* reads the sign on her cage. *Keep back! Do NOT offer food.* Jeffrey is an excellent keeper. He tosses her buns at regular intervals and before they left built a custom-made swing out of plywood and nylon rope that hangs, empty, above their kitchen table. The swing is for the twins and not for Gloria, but nevertheless she's very glad it's there.

"Two steps down. We're almost there. Okay, now guess."

"Obese tropical hogs about to have litters?"

"Nope."

"Hippos, then."

"Close. Think Gloria before breakfast."

"Siberian tigers?"

Gloria presses her hands against her eyeballs. Slow-motion rainbow splatters appear. She could be six, humoring her idiotic sister. Cast iron benches with peeling paint skins, injection-moulded gorillas on the ends of key chains, the arousing scent of their mother's tanning oil … August, 1983: she and Elaine demolishing vanilla ice cream, making muscular teaspoons of their tongues.

"African hunting dogs!" announces Jeffrey, just as Gloria reopens her eyes. Wet, bloodied muzzles tear through offal.

"I thought you said an animal I could relate to."

"I was being ironic. You know, in a British way."

This trip is Jeffrey's version of a honeymoon yet so far Gloria hates everything she sees. Their guest house is freezing despite the heat, a tall, thin Georgian terrace in Bloomsbury, stealth-bombed by psychotic wood pigeons. And everyone is so very *nice*, the little old ladies who run the place patting her navel and offering extra cushions while fellow guests wink and simper, lewd.

"Hungry at all?"

"Of course I am," Gloria half screams.

"You wait here then. No point the two of us going." Jeffrey, bold in taupe shorts, treads lightly through the jungle of her hormones. An avid map reader and note taker, never will he admit to feeling lost.

And while her husband grows curiously small, Gloria endures a barrage of kidney-kicking. "I'll have a ham baguette, a Coke and a caramel shortbread …" she shouts after him, "Oh, and some chips and a decaf cappuccino." With luck he will bring her a little something extra, a live chicken or goat to gnaw on later. Meanwhile she must keep her teeth to herself.

Noon and six are ravenous hours. Right now it is approximately eleven forty and if Gloria doesn't eat in the next twenty minutes she fears she may commit a random act of cannibalism. Do African hunting dogs ever eat each other? What sorry creature did those ribs belong to, that thread of viscera dangling from a black-edged mouth? If only she could be thrown raw meat on a tray. Instead she has to suck furry Lifesavers, do her best not to stuff the whole tube in.

The air is thick, her belly a submarine, its extruded navel the perfect disguise for a periscope. While two little fat boys point and stare, their own torsos soft and drooping, curvaceous, she imagines her own two, sneaking a quick, oval peek. What will they think of light, out here on the surface? It won't be long before they are real, two blind beasts she must somehow clamp to her bosom. What if she ends up dropping one on the floor? To her left, beside the dogs, are two female pot-bellied pigs with ten or twelve snouts latched onto their bodies, their eyes dull, as if they've already been turned into bacon. Gloria feels shrink-wrap constrict her skin. Plastic boxes full of flesh: the skinned, boned body parts of red-blooded creatures. Men in white coats have sliced up her remains and repackaged them in attractive polystyrene trays. Meanwhile she needs to eat but has no mouth left. A black hole invisibly haunting the supermarket, she sucks up twisters of chicken legs, spits out the bones.

"Do you mind if I sit here?"

At your peril, thinks Gloria. Her neighbor, she notices, is also a soldier, and battle-weary, bra straps slung low over her upper arms.

"How are you doing in there? All right?"

"Crap, actually. But thanks for asking."

"I wasn't talking to you. I was talking to *him*."

He is an over-pumped air mattress of an infant, dangerously crinkly at the seams.

"How old is he?"

"Four months."

"Good God." How did the woman's pelvis avoid shattering? Her hips seem barely as wide as her son's mouth. As his gigantic head turns from side to side his mother whips out a bag of Smoky Bacon potato chips and starts stuffing herself with them and when the child fusses pulls out a soother, plugs his face with it and continues to eat.

"You have to eat while you can, otherwise you'd starve."

Gloria's right hand makes a grab for the stroller snack tray, closes around some fluorescent orange crackers.

"It took them forty-seven hours to get him out of me. In the end they had to use forceps. See these bumps?" The woman flips back the stroller hood, brushes her son's fluff away from his ears. High on his domed forehead are two small raised areas. "These are going to be horns some day."

The crackers crumble. Gloria's pelvis is reassuringly wide, but the books say it's all about the angle. A poor presentation and your kids are toast. There are other fears. Elaine once asked her to play Siamese twins. After tying their legs together they pulled on her sweater, allowed each other one arm each. It was fun at first, bonking heads, but eventually Gloria panicked, untied her leg, pulled out her arm and slithered out the bottom. Her leg had rope burns and Elaine's sweater was stretched beyond use.

What if she goes into labour here? Three-month premature twins are not unheard of. And a zoo is not that different from a hospital: people in overalls, bad smells. Gloria's tissues are waterlogged, her blood vessels swollen by an extra three pints of Type O blood. In 1983, before her parents separated, the four of them visited Edinburgh castle together. She remembers the Tattoo, an elephant defecating. Someone had to rush on with a shovel. Those fibrous turds somehow stole the show. And then at the zoo Mum was all brittle and tearful, unable to open the Tupperware tubs of sandwiches because of her new three-inch-long false nails. Meanwhile she and Elaine fell in love with the orangutans, begged Mum to let them bring one home. Their arms were too long, their eyes intolerably doleful.

The twins are motionless. Perhaps they have strangled each other.

Gloria is at a crossroads, equidistant from Exit and Butterfly World. She could walk away right now, disappear into the crowds and Jeffrey would never, ever be able to find her. She has the A to Z as well as the guidebook and Jeffrey can't tell his West End from his East. But that would be cruel, wouldn't it, not to mention stupid. Who else would care for someone so grumpy so well? Jeffrey claims to be totally excited. He even worships her varicose veins, insists on naming them after rivers: the Congo, the Loire entwined around her calves, the majestic Thames blue and high just above her right ankle.

"Take that, you little madam!"

Hand-on-backside slap resounds unanswerably. A sullen girl, aged about eight, pulls down her turquoise shorts to examine her bum.

"Say you're sorry! Why don't you say you're sorry?"

"Sorry, Mum."

"That's better." Satisfied, Mum reaches up inside her T-shirt, unhooks her bra and pushes the head of a newborn infant into her. The girl resumes a listless horse-like prancing, up and down, up and down, up and down.

The woman beside Gloria is now in some kind of fugue state, eyes glazed, cheeks scattered with chip crumbs, while her little boy pulls rhythmically on his soother with the same kind of pleasure a man shows smoking a pipe. Jeffrey crushes her knuckles. A cold, sticky ultrasound probe makes its way across her torso. Here, the technician mumbles, your children's hearts.

Gloria salivates, gulps down air. Penguins make good fathers. If only Jeffrey could take a turn on the eggs. Instead he is forced to watch, helpless, an accomplice. No wonder he wants to feed her all the time.

"Jeffrey!" She has to find him. Talk about low blood sugar. Her urine would turn one of those pH sticks to dust. She staggers over to the nearest enclosure, where a man in a suit pulls red scarves out of his sleeves.

Gloria presses her face to the glass. Whiskery crones pick fleas out of each other's sideburns. Slack, rubbery jaws masticate fruit. *Today's Specials: Chicken Balti, Sticky Toffee Pudding.* Jeffrey is bending down to pick up a napkin. After he retrieves it he turns and waves.

"Be with you in a sec!" he mouths, and she glimpses his birth mark, the one shaped liked Atlantis, or what Atlantis might look like, were it located on the back of a white man's neck.

"Cheddar and pickle: that's for you. Also, the ginger lemonade and the fruit cake. I'm afraid they didn't have any red meat."

"That's fine."

Jeffrey relaxes. "Cheers!"

"Cheers."

Gloria inhales and thinks about PG Tips, her favorite teabags: those chimpanzees never wanted to star in commercials. No one asked if they liked wearing high heels and skirts. No one asked if they drank tea. *No one asked.*

One day soon she will eat raw dirt, scoop it up in perverse handfuls.

One day soon two skulls will ignite her cervix, the second following swiftly after the first. One day soon she will give birth to two human beings and never ever be able to explain how bad, yet good this felt, either to Jeffrey or to anyone else.

A Little Winter

HITCHING INTO TOWN in the early hours, she imagines the four of them, radiation sick, building a nuclear shelter out of sheet metal, boys with fragrant scalps pressed against her body, a kind of springtime anti-nativity play. The camp still in her clothes, her nails, her hair, she hunkers down in the back of a blue Ford Escort, notices her treachery: she's on the run. This evening, without luggage, she walked out of the camp as casual as anything. Not that there is any shame in leaving: women often come and go, taking breaks and coming back. But she is expected back tomorrow morning. The struggle within her to stay finally lost just as she is elected Gate spokeswoman.

As night skids past, Jen remembers other, less conscious battles, how the kids once fought her hard and how she tamed them, broke them almost with her slaps, her words. The challenge had been Joel: the parts of him that lay hidden. She had to move into his home, become indispensable, otherwise he'd never let her see. But then one morning she found herself marooned, stuck in a house with two angry boys. Caught between fear and desire, she slapped them both soundly, and from that moment on just could not stop. Opening the flaps of her tent last night at the peace camp, her right palm stung and burned as if in remembrance.

"There's no one home."

She is standing at the front door, dawn breaking.

"What do you mean?"

"They moved out. Place is being renovated." The woman in a wraparound apron looks somewhat familiar. Yes: old Mrs. Whitman, the baker of jam tarts, who brought a plate round once, full of curiosity, and was offered a hash brownie in return. Jen can't remember who laughed most, the kids or Joel.

"Oh, I see." Why does she feel surprised?

"Stark raving bonkers, he was. Poor wee lads, I felt sorry for them. Someone should have called the social."

Mrs. Whitman smiles; Jen turns away, her corrugated shelter collapsing. After the neighbour has gone back inside she walks around the back, past a cement mixer, begins to dig desperately in the soil. Where did she bury it? Was it here? The ugly, cherry-red vinyl of her portfolio, filled with grandiose projects and dead flies.

It's not the broken bones, but the resentment. No, her wounds have long since healed, replaced by unkind gossip as the price she now pays for that mad night. *What a martyr. She thinks she's better than the rest of us.* Unpeeling dried porridge skin from the bottom of each blackened pot, Jen craves something simple: a drink and a cigarette. Not scalding peppermint tea, not a soggy rollie, but two fingers of Jack Daniels in a proper glass and propped beside it a Marlboro in a tinfoil ashtray, a man with his legs crossed sitting not quite opposite, cruel wisecracks sputtering out of his mouth. She would listen, give as good as she got, all the while touching up her lipstick. The return of makeup: wouldn't that get them talking! It's sleeting here on the common and almost Christmas, except that hereabouts they call it Solstice. The best Jen can hope for, she thinks, is pneumonia, bad enough to land her in the General where four walls and a roof, hot food and indoor plumbing are still on offer. The Peace Camp is bare bones, most of the women escaped back to cities and families, those who are left, hardcore politicos or else like her, adrift and basically indigent, engaged with each other in psychological warfare, although few would go so far as to name it such.

At South Gate treading on worms is considered violent. Here at East, most protestors carry mace. But these are not issues to quarrel over. What matters now, the ground half frozen, donations at an all-time low and even the leftwing media departed, is food and warmth.

Last night a girl named Zef shoved her tattered blanket into a bin bag and fled without saying goodbye. After she'd gone, Jen scarfed her soup and a politico by the name of Marcy muttered:

"All it takes is a little bit of winter to separate the sheep from the goats."

"Speak for yourself." Soon the two of them were at it, full tilt. Closing her ears, Jen leaned back and at that moment a searchlight went off at the airbase. The night sky was unrelieved by stars.

Stubbing out her last smoke she had decided she would stay until Easter. But today the urge to run has become insurmountable. Joel will never forgive her for disappearing but she hopes that he will still be glad to see her; the boys, too, Leroy in particular, despite all the damage she once did them. She drops a wooden spoon. It has been a year.

Miranda comes and goes, busy with the parish she tends alongside her husband, who cares not a whit about Miranda's lovers, even those with spiky purple hair. Rose stays too, divorces her husband, telephones her sons every day: Eat your cabbage! Have you done your homework? Don't forget to change the guinea pig's hay. Ignoring Joel, Jen sends the boys birthday cards and presents: a box full of excellent conkers, the remains of a robin's egg, items she knows will be hated, just like she is, for not being perfect, permanent, or worth much; wonders if their mother has returned, the woman she attempted to replace, all Jen knows of her the vintage cocktail dresses lined up in Joel's wardrobe like alternate lovers. Here at the camp mothers are revered. Yet at East Gate there are no children, and all the women seem secretly glad of that.

"Isis, Astarte, Hecate, Demeter ..."

Slowly, portentously Jen lights each candle, just as she has been taught to do. Her tent mate unravels the purple wool, stretches it out to encompass all twenty women, weave a thrown spider web between them. For five months Jen cleaned out the toilets. Now she cooks. It's a perilous life, and one lived close to the bone in winter, but the promise of combat keeps her here and she has learned to hide her cynicism, convert it into wit. Marx and Black Sabbath have been unseated, replaced by the Great Mother and Holly Near. Tonight she is even leading the cleansing, the honesty circle that presages every action, an honour which means she has become a sister despite her aversion to such terminology. Jen's parents said they were disappointed. Why was she going to art school? Why not a serious profession? Didn't she know what they'd gone through for her?

"Rose?" Jen passes her the talking stick, a hazel wand wound about with embroidery silk.

"Thanks." Rose sighs, no longer the ingénue. Bundled up in army fatigues she barely resembles the cheeky runaway of April. Jen adjusts her hood, her brown roots grown in, wonders if she, too, has lost her enthusiasm. Not that she ever really had it to start with.

"Guess what, ladies: West Gate and North Gate have elected leaders." Rose pauses, to let this horror sink in. "And according to Indigo and Bett we should do the same. But I don't think …" Tears thicken her voice. "That, as women, *women*, we deserve this. Hierarchy is what we oppose. It represents patriarchy, everything we're resisting. We don't need leaders. Consensus is working just fine."

Rose passes the talking stick back around the murmuring circle while Jen feels a wave of nausea rise from her stomach. The truth is there are already leaders. Arguably she is turning into one. And the consensus Rose is glorifying, lubricated by apathy, the ground-down, exhausted state of most of the women, who would rather be asleep than at a meeting, any meeting, is no longer working, never has. Still, Jen must proceed.

"Thanks, Rose. Anyone else have an issue?"

Silence.

"Okay, fine. Now, for the action: the Spinners have decided they should go first, throw their webs over the wire, followed by the Songbirds. Meanwhile the women at North Gate plan to drum."

She can talk strategy like the best of them, recites slogans daily, backwards and forwards: time our in peace; war not love make – as if by playing games she resists believing, can still turn tail any time. Yet the facts do shock, not just the presence of deadly missiles but the relentless attempts by locals to evict the women, the murder, even, of one of their number, run over by a police van in suspicious circumstances. Such injustice burns her throat and scalds her into action, dear little Jennifer, her father with his hands around her neck or throwing a soft-bodied doll against the wardrobe and standing vigil, watching its vinyl head, concave after impact, pop back up and out, as if it lived.

"On this night of the dead, give us strength, Mother."

Leroy bites her back while she does the dishes. Damian puts cold porridge in her shoes. Jen tries so hard not to blow it's as if she's inflating, filling the kitchen like some great bladder a tiny pinprick will cause to rip and explode.

'Are we ready, women?"

They extinguish the fire, return to their tents for an hour of silent warmth. Jen wakes up suddenly, horrified that she may have slept in. But when she gets outside the others are waiting. Hugs are exchanged, fists gripped. An owl flies past. Then through the crackling dark they approach the perimeter. Knitted blankets are piled on top of barbed wire. Jen snags her sock, swiftly and deftly untangles it. The ground on the other side is forgiving, soft. A group of twenty makes it over the top, walks up the foreign slope towards the silos, the containers they regard with such personal hate it's as if they are intimately related. Jen is second in line. No one speaks. Neither do they use flashlights. Up above are stars and a full, yellow moon. The security patrol – two soldiers – is at the distant end of their march, far enough, they hope, not to hear anything, see their silhouettes until they are up there. Last time they only made it a few yards. Eight were arrested, six ended up in prison. This time they are better prepared. A legal team is on high alert.

Climbing the slope, Jen feels like a kid, almost giggling with the thrill of it, this crazy pilgrimage of ex-wives, drop-outs, although the danger of being shot at is real. The only drug she craves now is danger, truth's utter centre, that happy drunk when her bloodstream hums with hunger, the possibility of hope altogether the same now as desperation, her mind so full of nuclear threat that life without it would seem tarnished. She pictures herself being shot at; her parents, grieving. Stumbles over a thick, fat clump of nettles. Their leaves brush against her exposed knee.

"Ouch!"

"Ssh."

Shit, they have been spotted. As prearranged, the women break into a run and race through the floodlights, reaching the silos just as the military vehicles screech into action, clambering, breathless, up the slippery ladders. One woman falls; cries as she lands. Jen makes it up to the top and dances wildly, drops to her stomach as bullets whistle past. Or are they goose wings? Everything heading south now, getting out of here.

"Come down slowly. Do not resist arrest." Down below the police in gauntlets and helmets, their vehicles all amber flashing lights. Suddenly Jen realizes she's the only one up here. The others have all been arrested after climbing down so quietly she did not hear them: but they made it up! That's what she yells, screaming into the dark the fact of their triumph.

"We did it!" At that very moment sees beneath her the outline of a child's splayed body, falls.

That first night, they celebrate. Once the buses have left, the residents get down to business: cooking great pots of stew over fires, welcoming new recruits with ragged bouquets. Jen is feted with lentils, yogurt burgers. Someone gives her a down-filled sleeping bag. Later she is given boots and a sweater, the names of all the women in confusing sequence. Faces stare, intermittent in firelight, and soon she has decided not to question the logic of her arrival here on earth.

It's only when she crawls into bed, stinking of wood smoke, that the pictures of her father and Joel begin to proliferate, overtake her such that she wishes for whisky, something spiked and potent to kill her dreaming, terror of herself what shames her most. I'm afraid for the children. I'm afraid for the planet. The voices of the women around the campfire taunt her with anger. What's she afraid for? Films of herself grow faded and bleach out, jerky little movies of adolescence, a soft-sided bag dumped into a bin full of Leroy's letters to his mother, even her Portfolio of Horrors buried three feet deep in Joel's back garden, a place she intends to return to, sooner or later, assuming that Joel and his sons are still living there. Perhaps they have left already, or are coming after her. She imagines them driving in under military camouflage, radioactive with bitterness and need. Later, much later, when she finds them, Joel in a flat furnished with flea-ridden mattresses, the boys with foster families, "in care," she will remember the sharp chill this moment, consider it the beginning of her life as a goat.

Marmite sandwiches, cocoa, Ritz crackers with Stilton: the morning she arrives it's sunny and warm, the perfect weather for a ladies' picnic. Miranda is a vicar's wife, dressed in thick gumboots, Rose freckled and bosomy, a shopper in bulk.

"I told them I was just popping out to Sainsbury's! Just walked right out of the house and onto the bus." Rose and Miranda laugh, exchange glances; Jen shivers, discreetly alien, rolls up her sweatshirt to examine bruises, little finger marks along her ribs.

Rose the buxom lights up a fragrant cigarillo. "So when does the show start?"

Jen shrugs. She really doesn't know.

"Excuse me girls, but this isn't pantomime theatre." Miranda glowers. "Witness the paddy wagons."

Jen looks at them. Dogcatcher-mobiles. The coach that pulled up outside the shops was plastered with signs reading "peace" and "women only." While her seat mate ranted on about proliferation, Jen leaned back and explored the flip-up footrest. All she wanted was company, a destination. Only now does she feel fraudulent, as if even the fact of her femaleness were suddenly suspect. Will there be a vaginal inspection? What if hers does not pass muster? Joel's sons once demanded to see it, and she, stoned and silly, capitulated. Joel can hold that against her, if he wants.

"What are your politics?" demands Miranda.

"I don't have any."

"I voted Liberal until I read Andrea Dworkin." Rose stubs her smoke out and grins.

When pressed, Jen normally describes herself as anarcho-syndicalist. This usually shuts people up. But the truth is at twenty-three she has grown tired of black. Now she's a refugee, a battered woman, Joel the one who gave her a black eye this time, instead of a brass bed post, the pub floor. Plates of uneaten chips, Monopoly tantrums, smoke rising up like souls from the couch: she knew she had to leave, to escape through a window, crawl out with a bag of unwashed clothes and never mind the art buried in their back garden, its funeral one she'd presided over herself. That was early on, when they'd just got together, the art school dropout and the older man, the two of them busy cremating resumes, portfolios while the kids set fire to magazines, plush cats.

"And is this your first time?"

Jen nods. It's a lie of course. She's no demo virgin. Years of protesting fox hunts and picketing sex shops left her cynical and burned out. Meeting Joel, pretending to mother his offspring, gave her an excuse to shift her focus. Together they were all about beating the system, but when Joel turned to crime there was not much left: spanking, smashing Lego towers on principle, matriarchy reduced to stepmother wickedness. Little bags of coke tucked into film canisters.

"I was at Aldermaston, back in '58," continues Miranda. "Liddy and I, we've been tireless, honestly. A pain in the government's bloody proverbial. Of course Liddy died, silly cow, just after Christmas. Pancreatic cancer, bloody awful."

Miranda wipes real tears from her cheek.

"I'm very sorry."

But of course she isn't. This camp with its shamble of tents and tarps suddenly seems so utterly fucking bourgeois she feels like setting fire to its inhabitants despite the blue-black CND symbol tattooed on her inner wrist.

"Well I'm here to save my children." Rose folds her arms around her chest. "I don't want them buried by nuclear fall-out. It's the men, you know. My husband was in the army. He thinks deterrence works. But if you ask me it's just penis envy. Mine's bigger than yours!" Rose wiggles her hips.

"Right." Jen closes her eyes. She has a headache, forgot that running away would mean going cold turkey. Not that she's a junkie, not like Joel, but the booze and pills will take some time to get over, not to mention crushing maternal guilt.

Rose and Miranda have linked arms. Jen follows them over to the perimeter, where in an hour women are to gather, stare down US soldiers, sing and weep. Jen shrinks, tries to turn into a fencepost. Perhaps she should leave. But that would look bad. She's stuck. She has to stay here. Perhaps, like sex, the feelings will kick in later. And after all she's seen it on TV: rainbow scarves, baby clothes, women lying down in front of missiles. All very moving.

A woman in a beret shoves song sheets at them.

Rose gestures vaguely at some children. "Isn't that sweet? Perhaps I should have brought mine."

"Darling, I didn't know you had a family …"

Jen's companions disappear into the crowd.

"Take the toys from the boys …"

What was the common like before this, before the military arrived with their soldiers and guns? Jen imagines a green, tangled space filled with songbirds where local villagers take their pigs to graze. As a child she rode her bike through a quarry. Now she wishes she could find her way back. But for all she knows it, too, now has a fence around it, her parents long since become city residents, their civil war fueled by loneliness and roof leaks the council refuses, on principle, to mend.

"Which side are you on, girls, which side are you on?"

The police start to take up their positions. Piling out of vans, they look inhuman, a disciplined mass of black punctuation, ready to be dispersed amongst the crowd. Confrontation: excellent. Jen feels better. Fighting is one thing she can still understand.

Flat on the ground, face up. A position she knows all too well. Now look, here come the nasty missiles: Cubist-camouflaged and hung with netting. Close your eyes and think of England, dear. Men in uniform, their hands tight, one pair at her wrists, one at her ankles: she could be drunk or stoned, a half-dead prostitute, some sort of animal carcass left on the motorway, a victim they will wash their hands after touching, for all the respect she sees in their crayon-blue eyes. Nevertheless she likes it, this game of pretending: I am dead a coal sack you can deliver me, dump me on the verge along with the others until I stand up and shudder, return to the protest.

The slap of fresh dough: nights spent listening to her father's fists connect with her mother's flesh and make comfort of this. Her own private torture of kittens and field mice, night-time visits to the limestone quarry, where she buries their corpses under gravel and whispers cruel prayers over each pit. Pink clouds shaped like buses or traction engines, photographed with a dodgy Instamatic then stored inside her Portfolio of Horrors, a crimson vinyl vanity case she chucks dead flies into, flies she kills with a rolled-up newspaper and records in Roman numerals along its side. She is thirteen, sixteen, seventeen, eighteen. Folders of A4 pages, covered with poetry, old Mrs. Pinkerton's hands, plump and dimpled, reaching out just that bit too fast to grasp them, as if they were some relic of Rimbaud's. Jen the focus of too many caring teachers, their ambitious attempts to save her from her parents, until she heads off to art school and finds a lover, someone who can wallop her in style: meanwhile down with pornography! Save the foxes! Brilliant collage of newspaper headlines, charred roaches. Abuser ditched in favour of craggy Joel who convinces her that paint is a capitalist substance. Better use blood: Joel-and-the-boys, drug-dealer plus bastard offspring the perfect mock family to exchange for her parents, whose refusal to kill each other grows mordant, tiresome. Leroy a bone-handled knife piercing woodwork, his brother a brown rubber sphere, slamming walls, Jen's desire to crush both without warning, e.g. breaking Leroy's race track into pieces because he annoyed her by sitting watching Dallas, e.g. kicking Damian in the back.

"We are gentle, angry women ..."

Lifted again and again, she pretends this is exactly what she came for: to champion peace despite her all-black clothing, the safety pins that dangle off her sleeves. Soon Rose is also protesting, stretching her gorgeous body out like a lion's. Her twins are boys and for that reason were not welcome.

"I'm not going back!" she yells to Jen, ecstatic. Jen, horizontal, thinks of ways to smear that smile from her face.

Something About the Animal

S HE ALWAYS HAS SUGAR CUBES. Sometimes an apple too, if she can steal it, her mother very particular about the fruit bowl, perhaps because they can barely afford to fill it, the apple she has tonight a real beauty, evenly coloured green and red. She feels his tongue and lips as he cracks it eagerly. His teeth are long and yellow, almost comical. His nose is warm and soft and speckled with dots. Once the apple is gone he asks for more by pushing his face into her empty pockets.

"I don't have any more, you big fat lump."

She knows what it feels like to go hungry, to spoon curried baked beans onto stale cream crackers and take as long as possible to eat them. She also knows the luxurious mischief of satiety, bursting Satsuma segments inside her mouth until the kitchen table is a whirl of shed skins. But this less so. Her life so far lived out between these boundaries, the edge of not-enough always still raw.

The horse is old. His dark brown eyes are rheumy. His bones jut out and he favours one of his legs. No use to anyone, someone still keeps him, untethered in a meadow that surrounds a farm. Every evening for the past few weeks she has visited after tea, stayed until the sky is streaked with sunset, talking to the horse, telling him her troubles. And when she gets back to the house it's a little easier, her mother awake yet motionless before the television, as if all the life had just drained out of her, her mother not even noticing whether she's back or not.

Tonight, after the horse has finished eating, she climbs over the fence and into the field. While he stands, one foot tucked up gracefully, flicking his tail left and right, she runs her hands over his mottled coat. Beneath the hair she can see his skin. His sides are warm, cooler down by the knee, and she wishes she had brushes or curry combs, whatever it is they use to groom old horses, for his rough mane is knotted with burrs.

"We had English today. Debra Kelly read Viola in Twelfth Night and I was so jealous. I never get to read. She read *If music be the food of love, play on* and I thought of you, like whether you have ever listened to music. I could bring my violin down here but I'm not very good. I once read that pigs like listening to music. They get fatter. I'm vegetarian. Did I tell you that? So I would never, ever eat horse."

Her mother cooks fish fingers every Friday. She eats them but feels guilty about it. She bought a block of tofu once from a health food shop, plonked it on her plate that night and ate it, mouthful by disgusting, tasteless mouthful lifted to her lips on the back of a fork. These the kinds of facts that comprise her identity, blurred and inchoate as it is.

"I'll be thirteen next birthday." She and her mother never talk about it, what her mother does to make ends meet. "You're a good boy." She spreads her arms wide, holds the horse around the neck and kisses his withers. It's then that the boy appears.

"You're trespassing. This is private property." He sits down on top of the fence between them.

She shades her eyes to get a good look at him.

"What's your name?"

"That's none of your business. You should get out."

His voice is plummy, the speech of a spoiled brat. He is her height but, if possible, thinner. His clothes are odd, scruffy yet formal. He's wearing Jesus sandals.

"If this is your horse you should take better care of him. He's too thin and he needs to be groomed. He also needs his leg taken care of. Do you live here?" She points behind the boy, to the farm.

"Yes."

"I never see you."

"That's because I'm usually away at school."

"Oh."

"My dad's a lawyer. He could take you to court and get you imprisoned."

"He can't be lawyer *and* a farmer."

"Yes, he is. We have a flat in London. And a villa in Spain. All this," the boy sweeps his arm around majestically, as if to take in not just the field, but the river, the viaduct, the low hills beyond them, the sky, "all this is just a hobby."

"And so is he your hobby horse?"

"Don't be stupid. Lancelot is very old. We're probably going to have him put down this winter. He's lame, you know, so nobody can ride him. I have my own pony called Steam."

"Steam? That's a silly name for a pony."

"I like steam engines." The boy sounds defensive. "What do you like?"

"Nothing. I don't like anything." Suddenly she wants to leave. But to go now would be to concede defeat, so she leans back against the fence and strokes Lancelot's nose again, secretly glad he does not leave her for the boy.

"Look here, you know you are trespassing. So you should get out before I call my father. He has a shotgun."

The girl feels agitated, but she does not leave, even when Lancelot, having polished off all the sugar, walks away from her towards the farmhouse.

"Did you think I was joking about the shotgun? I swear I'm not."

"What are those?"

"These?" The boy glances down at his arms. They are horribly scarred. Long, purple lines extend from his wrists to his elbows, and when he looks up his face is harder, different. "These are from when I got mauled by a tiger. We were on holiday in India. I don't remember much about it. I was only small. Have you ever been to India? Where do you live, anyway? Down in the estate?"

Instead of replying she climbs up onto the fence. The stuffy air in their flat above the electrician's always smells of burnt toast and bananas; the air here is filled with the scent of lilacs, drifting over from beyond the farmhouse, mixed with hawthorn and elderflower, the stink of cow dung. After she sits down beside him, the boy glances back over his shoulder and she notices with a shock that he is pretty. His fair hair is almost white, his nose freckled. He looks like a doll, or a fairy, not a real person, a boy who in different clothes could be a girl.

"Come on, I'll race you!"

Without warning, he slides down into the field behind. Before he can beat her she takes off, past Lancelot, over the empty ditch and towards the elm copse. Once beneath the trees the air is clammy. A cloud of midges shivers above her head. There are other paths into the country, gates and stiles she navigates to reach the river, the slow, brown S-shapes of its progress out from the town and towards the distant sea. But where she stands right now is private, forbidden, its view magnificent. Oh, there are places she has visited on field trips, enormous houses stranded in yards of gravel, surrounded by terraces, gardens, greenhouses, orangeries, homes that once belonged to single families, families that owned whole villages, even towns. But this is the first time she has really sensed it, the possibility of owning property, of walking for miles and miles and never leaving home.

The boy jogs up beside her, points a finger. "My father says there used to be a gallows, right up on that hill, against the skyline. That's where they hung thieves. They took it down, though."

And for a thrilling moment she almost sees it, a body hanging awkwardly by its neck, the body of a man killed for a partridge, hanging right where the main road turns north.

"Look, there's Steam." The boy grips her shoulder, lifts her right arm until it points straight at the hills. At first she sees nothing. Then she spies the pony, a rust-coloured speck down beside a stream.

"He's my pony. Did I say that already? My father bought him for me when I turned twelve."

"Take me down there, then. Teach me to ride him."

The boy stares at her for a moment. "All right, I will."

But instead of waiting for him to take the lead she runs out of the copse and down to the river, stands alone on its crumbling bank and shouts: "Fuck you, Errol!" She didn't mean to say this.

"Who's Errol?" asks the boy, breathless. Instead of answering she throws in a pebble, proud of the way it skips almost to the other side. The river is pocked with the dimples of pond skaters. They stand still, watching, until someone back at the darkened farmhouse starts calling "Piers, Piers, it's time to come in!"

211

She does not return to the farm for several days. Instead she sits on the settee with her mother. Together they watch episodes of Dallas, laugh about the hairdos, share packets of crisps. It's fun but then her mother starts sighing, complaining of pains in her stomach, and takes to her bed.

The girl doesn't really want to, but she stays home from school, bringing her mother orange squash and aspirin, sitting beside the phone in case it rings. She thinks about the boy while doing the dishes, wonders if he has a nanny, a maid. What must it be like to go to boarding school? Does he ever get to talk to girls?

By the third evening her mother is better. There are lots of messages, so her mother spends a lot of time on the phone.

"I'll go back to work tomorrow," she says. "Then Errol's coming over on the weekend."

Errol is her mother's lover. He used to be her client but that changed. Errol is a Caribbean taxi driver. He lives in Manchester and drives over on Sunday afternoons. When he visits her mother wears her good dress, emerald green with a low neck and floaty, paints her lips, ties her hair up and for a few hours comes back to life. The two of them sit in the living room and sip rum and Coke while Errol plays highlife music on the record player. Sometimes they even dance and the girl watches, embarrassed to see her mother so in love.

There's nothing really wrong with Errol. He's handsome and funny, his parrot-patterned shirts and twisty dreadlocks associated in her mind with coin tricks and knock-knock jokes. Errol is the only man who visits her mother, but no one around here misses anything. *Does he have a long dick? Does it reach his knees?* The kids at school know what her mother does. She cannot change that. But Errol also has a wife and kids back home in Saint Lucia, is planning to bring them out here, to live in his flat.

The girl has only been there once: Errol, her mother and she sitting around laughing at Errol's bad jokes, stuffing themselves with okra, fried plantain, salt fish ackee. She scanned the place for photos, couldn't find any. The feeling in her stomach when she left was the one she once had at the top of a rollercoaster, knowing the only way back down was steep.

"You look beautiful." She thinks he's addressing her mother, but he means her. She blushes, furious, busies herself arranging Rich Tea fingers on a cracked plate.

"Here's a tenner, sweetheart. Go out and buy yourself some little treat."

She takes the crumpled bill, forces a smile. She knows the money isn't meant for her, at least not all of it. But if he gives it direct to her mother, she freaks out.

Sometimes, after walking around the town, buying a Coke or a Fanta and window shopping, the girl sneaks home early to listen to them fucking. The sounds they make both beautiful and dreadful. She has to stuff socks in her mouth to muffle her laugh.

When she reaches the farm she hears shouting: boys in high spirits, the splash of swimming. She follows the fence until it opens up into a driveway, walks all the way to the front door of the house. She knocks quietly at first, then loudly, when no one answers goes around the side, where a path opens up into a garden.

Two boys the same age as Piers, one red headed, the other dark, hold his head underwater. Just when she fears the worst they let go and Piers bursts out like a salmon. The scars on his arms are livid. The two others laugh. She walks towards them, between beds of blue and purple flowers, up to the concrete rim of the aquamarine pool.

"Stop that! Stop trying to drown him!" Where are his mother and father? Tall French windows open onto the patio but she can see nothing behind them, only the scene in front of her, reflected back.

"What-what are you-doing here?" Piers's breath rattles. He holds onto the concrete rim and gasps. "It-it's only a game."

"I thought you were going to teach me to ride."

Instead of answering, Piers hauls himself out of the swimming pool, grabs a thick, white towel and dries off. Then he runs a hand through his spun gold hair. Once it is slicked back he grins at her, cocky. She feels foolish. Perhaps she should never have come in.

"So who are you then, Piers's girlfriend?" The red-haired boy has little, wobbly titties. The two boys guffaw.

Piers blushes. "I didn't think you were going to come today."

"Yeah, well." Her voice tails off. Suddenly she feels self-conscious about her appearance. Once she had a feather cut but it's grown out. Short hair is expensive. So are new clothes. Most of hers stink of second-handness, no matter how many times they're washed. Today she is wearing red shorts and an off-white t-shirt. There are spots on her forehead, dark brown hairs on her legs.

"I'm sure you know by now that Piersy's a pansy. He gets up to all kinds of mischief when he's at school."

The dark haired boy makes flat-footed water footprints over to the French windows, opens one and goes inside. Soon the redhead follows, smirking and mincing.

Piers says nothing, just drapes the towel around his shoulders and goes in too.

Inside it's dark, too dark to see. She stands motionless, terrified. Should she take her shoes off? Before she has time to decide the boys reappear. One holds a couple of riding hats under his arm. They march straight past her, out into the sun again, Piers following behind, avoiding her eyes.

The boys walk through a gate at the bottom of the garden, over to a cobbled yard. The yard is scattered with hay and on one side are stables.

"Listen, I'm not supposed to ride when my parents are out. But they won't be back until four so we have some time. Rufus, I suggest you take Merlin. We could have a contest."

Merlin is a slim black horse, with a star on his forehead, and something about the animal quiets the boys down. They seem less mischievous, their voices softer and their movements slower as Piers leads her out onto the cobblestones. The girl can see how young the pony is, how fit and supple. Standing beside her, Piers looks taller, stronger.

"She's a beaut," says the red head.

"My dad has six race horses, but we never see them. He says they're just an investment. I think he might get me a pony though, if I ask." When no one responds, the dark boy glances at her sideways, runs his eyes up and down her body and then looks away. Unsure what to think, she holds her breath for five seconds, watches Piers pull up a big square piece of stone.

"This is our mounting block. It was my grandmother's. She used to have it on her property in Kent." Piers climbs up it and onto Merlin. The dark-haired boy jumps up behind him. "Steam's out in the meadow. You can help me catch her." He kicks the horse's side. It obeys his command.

"Wait for us!"

The girl is angry. She can see now that she is irrelevant. He is getting the horse out to impress the others, to prove to them that they need him, that he is desirable. The swimming pool was not enough. But she will not give up.

Out in the meadow it's far more spacious and wild. Cow pats, horse dung and grass tufts make the terrain complicated to cover, so everyone shuts up, all of them walking apart. The dark-haired boy has come down off Merlin. Piers is now cantering alone across the field.

"Get out of the way."

"Jesus Christ, he's a loony!" The red-head grabs her and pushes her down as Piers gallops past then executes a smooth turn, and it's then she sees the strange arrangements of posts set up at the other end of the meadow. Steam clears them all, one after the other. When he pulls up beside them, Piers is breathless.

"She's a damn fine pony," says the red-head. "But now it's my turn."

Piers dismounts and hands over the reins. The boys shake hands as the red-head stuffs a riding hat onto his head and sets off across the meadow, and suddenly she sees that they are all riders, their contest not about who can stay upright but who can clear the fences, gallop fastest, that she will not get a chance. She has saved him from drowning and put up with his rudeness, not even caring that he barely acknowledged her, all so she can get close to his horses and now he won't even let her try.

"Oh, bad luck!"

The red-head has just knocked a pole off. It rattles hollowly as it hits the ground.

Instead of caring she turns and makes her way back towards the river, to the shallow ford she knows she can cross back over to the elm copse, where the old white horse is standing, his face turned away.

"I don't have any sugar cubes," she tells him, then remembers an old boiled sweet stuck in her pocket. It's lime green and covered in fluff but she offers it to him, anyway, and as he eats it she walks back against the fence. It's easy to jump. Soon she is mounted. Lancelot begins to walk, transferring his weight from one hip to another. She feels the unevenness in his gait.

She presses her legs in. He interprets this as a command and begins to go faster, his back a rollicking, slippery seat but she hangs on. The hot mass of his flesh underneath her enough of a distraction she doesn't notice as they trot through a gate into the driveway that a car is pulling up in the road ahead.

Lancelot whinnies. He bucks. The car is in front of them. A man and a woman sit inside. The horse does a strange sideways dance and she dangles from his back, slides off it into the shrubs that line the fence and the horse is gone now, cantering back to his field, car doors slamming, voices suddenly loud. She gets up before the man leaps the gate and when he reaches her she is shaking but unhurt, yet before she can even speak he has slapped her and slapped her, taken hold of her elbow and thrown her sideways. Her temple cracks on concrete and for a moment there is nothing, then everything, the sun hot. She feels sick and dizzy. This must be the lawyer. He is tall and broad, red in the face, fair hair hanging smoothly over strong cheekbones. Behind him the woman gets out of the car, high heels crunching across gravel, unlatches the gate and closes it behind her. Her dress is white, her tanned legs muscular.

"What the bloody hell is going on?"

The man is looking at her, but he is not talking to her.

"Where's Piers?"

"They're only boys, Lucas."

The woman's voice is taut, strangled. She clutches a bag decorated with large buckles, holds it across the front of her dress while sweeping strands of hair out of her eyes. She stays there, just inside the gate while her husband marches off behind the farmhouse. His voice is loud and fascinating, still audible when he reaches the meadow where the girl imagines him knocking the boys off their horses, dragging them back to the house by their ears.

"Rufus told me Piers is a pansy."

The woman starts. "What did you say?"

The girl does not repeat her message. Instead she slowly gets to her feet, shakes off the gravel. The woman is only an inch or two taller than her.

Later, when she comes back to the farm, she will come with a different kind of knowledge, the result of evenings spent with some of her schoolmates, bribing adults to buy them booze, will know then that she has some kind of power: to lure boys, to bring them to their knees, and soon after that will turn her back on the country, on rivers and fields, laneways and distant gallows, will travel far, give birth to children, feed them well yet fear them for their beauty, before all that will discover terror, not the kind you feel but the kind you incite. She will no longer be a child who carries sugar but a woman who understands duplicity, the agility required to dance, to escape. Errol will be gone, her mother adrift. But first she will be driving past in the passenger seat of a car belonging to a handsome, ambitious man, and as he pulls in, happy to find a place where they can be private, she will recognize the outline of the farmhouse, the uneven slats of the fence she once leaned into.

"Let's go somewhere else," she will say, but the man will not listen, so hungry will he be for her body, for that which he has coveted at a distance, so he will push her against the fence and nudge her head back, and she will parry his kisses with her own.

But for now she is standing, watching the woman open her buckled handbag and take out an engraved flask. While the woman sips, her eyes close, her eyeballs darting back and forth behind painted lids.

"You should go now," she says, "before he comes back."

But the girl doesn't move. Instead she feels the side of her head with her fingertips, aware that there is blood but not too much. Her own mother sometimes comes home with bruises, little telltale marks on her neck or her face. What does this woman have, other than houses?

"Lucas, Lucas come here. Oh my God."

The man has appeared from around the side of the farmhouse. The girl shrieks, but it's not her he's after, he barely sees her, marches over to the gate and into the field. Piers's face appears then disappears in the farmhouse window. He is probably crying. But this is not what she will remember, three years later, pressed into the fence. First she will recall the shot and how it echoed, bouncing off the walls and then the hills, and only later will she remember what came before this, before the horse was murdered in its field: the expression on the father's face as he walked right past her, a double-barreled shotgun pressed up against him, as if it were the only thing he loved.

Acknowledgments

The poem fragment on page 180 is a line of Rumi's translated by Coleman Barks from *The Essential Rumi*, Castle Books, 1997.

Some of these stories previously appeared in the following:
"Keeping Mum" *The Malahat Review*.
"A Special Sound" *Descant*.
"Floaters" *Grain*.
"Beryl Takes a Knife" and "Something About the Animal" *The New Quarterly*.
"A Little Winter" *Best Canadian Stories 2010*, ed. John Metcalf (Oberon Press).
"Going to India" *Ars Medica*.
"The Stockholm Syndrome" www.joyland.ca.

Thanks to the Canada Council, David Bergen and the Humber School for Writers, Robyn Read, Kim Jernigan, Robin Roger and the editors of all the magazines and anthologies these stories have appeared in (as well as some they have not). Thanks also to Cynthia Flood, Susan Leibik, Olga Broumas, Nancy Pollak, Fiona Tinwei Lam, Lydia Kwa, Barbara Parkin, Maggie Ziegler and Ora Wayne Hughes. Thanks to all my students. Thanks to Freya (wow, Mom!) Thanks to Gabrielle Nouveau for her incredible images and Daniel Henshaw for the photograph. Special thanks to Dan Wells, and a huge thank-you to John Metcalf, whose letter arrived at exactly the right time.

About the Author

DANIEL HENSHAW

Cathy Stonehouse was born and raised in the UK and emigrated to Canada in 1988. She holds a BA in English from Wadham College, Oxford and an MFA in Creative Writing from the University of British Columbia. Between 2001 and 2004 she edited the award-winning literary journal *Event* and in 2008 co-edited the creative nonfiction anthology *Double Lives: Writing and Motherhood* (McGill-Queens University Press). The author of a poetry collection, *The Words I Know* (Press Gang Publishers, 1994), her writing has also appeared in numerous magazines, newspapers and anthologies including *Dropped Threads 3: Beyond the Small Circle* (Random House, 2006), *White Ink: Poems on Motherhood* (Demeter Press, 2006) and *Best Canadian Stories 2010* (Oberon Press). A second poetry collection is also due out with Inanna Press in fall 2011. She lives in East Vancouver with her husband and daughter.

RECYCLED
Paper made from
recycled material
FSC® C103567

Marquis Book Printing Inc.

Québec, Canada
2011

Printed on Silva Enviro 100% post-consumer EcoLogo certified paper,
processed chlorine free and manufactured using biogas energy.